Michael Cyprian O'Byrne

Song of the Ages

A Theodicy, Books I and II, And other Poems

Michael Cyprian O'Byrne

Song of the Ages
A Theodicy, Books I and II, And other Poems

ISBN/EAN: 9783744772662

Printed in Europe, USA, Canada, Australia, Japan

Cover: Foto ©Andreas Hilbeck / pixelio.de

More available books at **www.hansebooks.com**

"He comes not back: O breaking heart be still!
While time endures woman shall endure."

Book II, p. 57

SONG OF THE AGES,

A THEODICY,

BOOKS I AND II,

And Other Poems.

—

BY M. C. O'BYRNE,

Of the Bar of Illinois.

—

So praye I to God that none miswrite thee.
Ne thee mysmetre for defaut of tonge.
(*Chaucer.*)

—

LA SALLE, ILL.,
H. E. WICKHAM, Publisher.
MDCCCXCVII.

PREFACE.

An eminent critic, Mr. Theodore Watts, has said that "what is demanded of the epic of art....is unity of impression, harmonious and symmetrical development of a conscious heart-thought, or motive."* Possessing this, and being conscious of it, the presumption is, therefore, that an epic poet is urged to "make" in some such manner as John Wesley's lay preachers were impelled to exhort. If an excuse or apology be desirable for such a work as is here offered to the reader, I can sincerely urge that at its inception I felt,—whether or not deluded time will tell,—assured of both a motive and an impulse. My scheme was, briefly, to

Vindicate the ways of God to Man

by tracing the latter from the first rude cradle, revealed to our wondering eyes by Science, upward to that glorious consummation of the ages which it is so sad to be asked to contemplate as in turn certain to sink in endless night. That the impulse was not lacking is, I think, proved by another of Mr. Watts' measures, for I can honestly avow that during the progress of this work I felt as a child, "with ears attuned to nothing but the whispers of those spirits from the Golden Age who, according to Hesiod, haunt and bless the degenerate earth."

Painfully conscious, however, that in poetry, as in the religious life, there are false and misleading spirits, I launch my little barque upon an ocean where its qualities will be surely and swiftly tested, yet not without hope that this, our first adventure, may encourage us once more to put to sea.

The original design of a "Song of the Ages" comprehended a poem of at least four books. In deference, however, to a sentiment

---

*Encyclopædia Britannica, article "Poetry."

which seems to be almost universal,—namely, that the people of this generation have no time for epic poetry,—this intention remains, at least for the present, unfulfilled. The time, place, and manner of publication have been dictated by the logic of circumstances,—the *saeva paupertas* which has spared the world incalculable volumes of mediocrity. Two years ago arrangements had been made for issuing the work in London, the literary centre of the English-speaking world, but almost at the last moment it was withdrawn, the reason being that the author was required to sign a contract that seemed to him both illiberal and unjust. Having crossed the ocean twice, the book finds its birth in the place of its conception, where possibly it is fated to be buried. In one sense, however, the song and the singer are singularly favored: they are both free from the taint of that commercialism which, when it finds a place in literature as a controlling principle, is like the wide breaking in of the waters of desolation.

Now, Little Book, go forth in peace!

M. C. O'BYRNE.

La Salle, Illinois.
  March 10, 1897.

SONG OF THE AGES.

PRELUDE.

I.

De Profundis.

DE PROFUNDIS CLAMAVI! from the depths of my soul I cried,
Asking light from the darkness, where I wandered without a guide;
For the stars that twinkled above me they recked not of me or my prayer,
And the weight of a life that was wasted had burthened my heart with
    despair:
Asking light from the darkness, for the stars that shine in the sky,
Though questioned through countless ages, have never vouchsafed reply:
Listening in vain 'mid the silence for a voice that should pierce the gloom,
Watching in vain for the angel to roll the sealed stone from the tomb,
Where, wrapped in folded cerecloths, the weft that my hands had made,
My early hopes were buried, where my own dead Past was laid.
From the depths of my soul I pleaded till my mood was changed to scorn
Of the senseless god* that cannot resolve us why man is born.
Of brooding Brahm amorphous in whose thought the world began,
The god whose sole interpreter is Echo, the wife of Pan.
And weary and worn with thinking, I said I will live as one
Who recks not of the evil to follow the morning's sun;
I will drink of the cup of pleasure, I will hie me to Beauty's arms,
And renew my youth in dalliance at the wellspring of her charms,
My golden youth, my potent youth, when Function and Desire
Went hand in hand unto the shrine where glowed the Paphian fire.

---

    *Apparently oblivious of the purpose of this poem, a "clever" publisher's
reader objected that this and the succeeding lines were atheistic. It was scarcely
worth while to controvert so learned a Theban.

II.

Dixit Insipiens.

COME, let us live, my Lesbia! come, Lesbia, let us love![b]
The day is brief, the night is long, the things which are above
Our human ken concern us not, they only are the wise
Who know the good the hour affords and grasp it ere it flies.
Let Pentheus climb his tree to break th' impenetrable bars,
And spoil his sight to contemplate the sameness of the stars,
Their everlasting sameness, in that scroll we may not read
One word of thought or purpose on which man may hang a creed;
Naught but the tale mechanical, the everlasting round,
Vicissitude of energy, of space without a bound,
Or coast or shore or islets green wherein the soul may rest
As in the bosom of its God, the Islands of the Blest.
Come, Lesbia, turn thine eyes on me, with me defy the blind
Chance universe revealed to sense but not revealed to mind.
Come, let us drink our fill of love and make each present hour
Give forth its sweets as to the bee the nectar from the flower.
Twin soul of mine! though none may know what lies beyond the stream
Of time, or whether aught we see be other than a dream,
Our love is real; holding thee, I care not if the world,
The cinder heap of caecic Chance, be into chaos hurled.

(b) *Vivamus mea Lesbia, atq' amemus.*

III.

Exurgat Deus!

As lay Titanogene[2] the while its beak the vulture dyed
In blood and gall, so lay I when my Lesbia left my side.
O Sun, didst thou forbear to shine when I, in my despair,
Blasphemed thy light because the Lord of Life denied my prayer,
And claimed His own?   O crusted Earth, say, was thy granite shell
Convulsed when from my frenzied soul I cursed all Nature?   Tell,
Oh tell me all ye lucent orbs that sail æthereal seas
What shocks disturb their limpid calm when impious thoughts like these
Rush forth into infinity, to roll for evermore,
The billows of man's impotence, through seas without a shore?
There bound, but mutinous, I lay, and there, O Power Divine!
Thy love discovered me, there poured the healing oil and wine:
The veil was rent, the cumulus of doubt was thrown aside,
And with unclouded eye I saw my Maker justified.

    *   *   *   *   *   *

O Lord of Life, O Quickener! inspire my feeble lips
To tell the vision that I saw in that apocalypse!
Resolve the chaos of my mind as Thou of old didst spread
Thy wings o'er earth's proplasmic mist to vivify the dead!
Tune thou the poet's harp and teach his hand to strike the keys,
To show how the Arch-Poet makes celestial symphonies!

---

  [2]Prometheus, son of the Titan Iapetus and the nymph Clymene.

SONG OF THE AGES.

BOOK THE FIRST.

THE STONE AGE.

I.

Descend, ye stateliest of the dulcet choir
Whose haunt is by the sacred springs! descend,
Calliope and Clio, and inspire
This tale of Merops[3], haply it may blend
Myth, fantasy, and fable, as of old
The voices of the rivers and the trees
Commingled in that loftier story told
Of Ilion's fall by rapt Mæonides!
Forsake awhile the sacred mount, desert the hallowed ring
Trod by Apollo's feet, and aid your votary to sing!

II.

To sing of man primæval, man co-heir
With mammoth and with unicorn; his home
Theirs also, rocky caves and grottos where
The congealed crystals wrought on floor and dome,—
The archetypes of all his greatest work
In after ages,—column, gargoyle, frieze,
Buttress and span; his chief intent to lurk
Within some deep recess or shade of trees
In fearful hope and hopeful fear, yet resolute to tear
His weapons from the antlered elk, his raiment from the bear.

III.

Behold him, then, the primal man, in whom
There latent sleeps the godlike gift of mind,
Suspended, dormant, as within the womb
Of the great cosmic universe, combined
With metalloids and metals, in some cloud
Of distant world-stuff haply there may float
The fiery embryos of a radiant crowd
Of future world-kings, who in some remote
As yet chaotic sphere shall rise to reinforce the throng
Of those who round the great white throne shall chant the victor's song.

[3] Μέροψ, the voice-dividing, an epithet of man.

IV.

To him unknown as we have learned to know
Thy loveliness, O Maia! from his birth
The sport of wild convulsion—hail and snow,
The torrent's roar and the rude tempest's mirth,
These were his lullabies, while overhead
The rugged peaks, icebound, were rent and torn
By blasts from Phlegethon which seemed the dread
Voices of strident demons, who in scorn
Of helpless man their levin bolts in frolic fury whirled,
And shook in wanton play the props and pillars of the world.

V.

See where the troglodyte, his recking hands
Red with the current from his quarry's veins,
Betakes him to yon cave; see where she stands,
His partner, sharer of his joys and pains,
Primæval wife and mother; to her breast
She hugs her offspring, fortified with fold
And cincture of warm fur, love's forethought lest
The puny life should shrivel in the cold
Of this aphelial realm,—e'en here, despite the glacial breath,
Maternal love shines bright and clear, the love that conquers death.

VI.

My mother, O my mother! oft I deem
That thou art by my side,—what though the thought
Be but a fantasy, a waking dream,
Yet I encourage it, for doth it not
Present me with thine image?—not as when
I saw thee last in life, thy gaze withdrawn
To that near shore whose brilliant Pharos then
Bespoke the haven and allured thee on,—
Not thus, but as when in thy prime, tender and true and mild,
I see thee, mother, once again and am once more a child.

VII.

The soul will oft grow aged ere the clay
In which it is imprisoned doth attain
Its due development, because a day
May blight and make it sere; as when the grain
Falls wilted in the jagged lightning's track,
Or crushed beneath the cloudburst not to rise
Once more a golden plateau from the wrack
Of the fierce deluge, though autumnal skies
Gleam sapphire-like from dawn till eve,—and how shall hope survive
In tainted breasts where guilt and grief leave not the germ alive?

VIII.

But constant through the mists of rolling years,
Undimmed by time, uncankered by disgrace,
One hallowed form in memory's shrine appears,
One sacred icon nothing can efface,—
Thy mother's, child of sorrow!—bitter tears
Of blood perchance thy heart has shed since last
Her voice fell on thine ear, thy toils and fears
And sorrows have been many, but the past
Holds no remembrance that can move thy spirit like to this—
The memory of thy mother's look, the memory of her kiss.

IX.

And now, firm-treading o'er the rough moraine,
Comes the swart hunter laden with his spoil
Of sheep whose musky fragrance fills the plain
With that strong essence which the artful toil
Of later Byzantine[1] shall intermix
With mortar in the Holy Wisdom's pile,
Justinian's glory, where the crucifix
Fell blood-imbrued beneath the crescent, while
A martyr's and a patriot's death, the noblest end, was thine,
Last of thy race as of the Greeks, O gallant Constantine!

[1] In allusion to the legend that in building the cathedral of Saint Sophia musk was added to the lime in making mortar.

X.

Sweet home! though but a hollow in the cliff,
Or wattled hut, pile-founded in the mere,
As dear unto the protoplast as if
Its walls were marble, rising tier on tier
In storied elegance with all that art
Can give of strength and beauty: that is home,
In desert or in wildwood, where the heart
Still finds its centre wheresoe'er we roam;
The dearest spot on earth to man, where urged by love the soul
Turns always as the needle turns toward the mystic pole.

XI.

Better the cave, the implement of stone,
Lacustrine hut, and the rude couch of leaves,
Than factory and furnace, which have grown
To be man's social curse, where naught relieves
The dull routine, no harmonies assuage
The whirling dissonance of wheel on wheel,
And hope and love seem blotted from the page
Of Nature's volume: are there drugs to heal
The cankered sores of Industry, or tonics to restore
The vital fluid to its veins and cleanse it as of yore?

XII.

Call not that home where, in the city's slums,
The poor are herded in a grisly swarm;
Where one unsullied zephyr never comes
To fan the fevered forehead, or the warm
Pellucid beams from Him that walks on high[5]
Find unobstructed entrance, where the soul
Grows dwarfed and stunted in a prurient sty,
Necropolis of virtue, and the whole
Grim offspring of Gehenna's pit in raw putrescence swell,
Expanding in its foetid slime to copragoges of hell.

[5]Hyperion,—Walking above,—the sun-god.

XIII.

The thing that hath been shall be: write ye this
Sure proverb, nomothete, upon the walls
In senate and in forum; Nemesis
Herself is bound by fate, and naught befalls
The globe or man but by the fixed decree
Of Him whose thoughts are æons and whose touch
On the three world-keys, crust and air and sea,
Is rhythmic revolution, causing such
Mutations as the sages tell the polar-cycles bring
When the swerved index makes complete the equinoctial ring.[6]

XIV.

Antelial winters once again shall lock
Their adamantine fetters 'round the zone
Whose life is now exuberant, the shock
Hypogenous be heard, as when o'erthrown
Atlagenes[7] slid smoothly 'neath the wave,
Metropolis of millions; once again
The happy hyperboreans shall lave
Their feet in thermal fountains, and the fen
Resound with cry of hern and coot where now the Iceking reigns,
And towers and palaces arise to grace the fertile plains.

XV.

O welcome revolution, if it bring
To earth once more another golden age,
Like unto that the shepherd boy did sing,[8]—
At once the Muses' prophet, bard, and sage,—
On slopes of Helicon, the while his sheep
Cropped the green herbage by the Horse's Well,
Bright Hippocrene, or surveyed the deep,
Calm pool where Aganippe's waters fell,
And ruminating saw unmoved reflected flocks below,
Where every mirrored fleece shone back like piles of drifted snow.

---

[6]The precession of the equinoxes.
[7]Atlagenes, the assumed metropolis of Atlantis.
[8]The poet Hesiod.

XVI.

Thrice happy time, the golden age ere gold
Was aught but an adornment! Mother Earth,
Renew thy youth and beauty, as of old
Bring healthful children to a painless birth!
What though our marts, where man is bought by man,
Be ice-concreted and green glaciers glide
Where sewage-tainted rivers whilome ran
Their sluggish poison to the ocean's tide?
Perish the past if from its wreck we win a worthier wealth.
And man's lost birthright be restored of innocence and health!

XVII.

Survey we now the home, the parent nest
Of human fellowship, wherein the three,—
Rude husband, wife, and babe,—are gone.   The best
Of all man's later art is mimicry
Of what we here behold.   A lofty hall,
Resplendent with a myriad marvels wrought
In grandest symmetry on roof and wall,
Each web from Nature's factory a thought
Of the great Master Weaver, God, a product of the loom
Whose shuttle weaves for men and worlds birth, progress, death, and
    doom.

XVIII.

Look where the ruddy glow from yonder fire,—
Assiduously fed—for heat is dear
To man unclothed by Nature,—turns each spire
And bulb of stalagmite to gold; the near
Columnar crystals gleam like rubies, while
The farther stalactites seem draped in bands
And scarfs of varying bronze, as in the aisle
Or nave of some great church each pillar stands
A column bound with rainbow rings when at the close of day
Through many a rare and pictured pane the level sunbeams play.

XIX.

Midway within the grotto gleams a fount,
A silvery basin without duct or course
Of visible supply, its verge a mount
Of alabaster like to that whose source
Is found near well-springed Thebes; many a form
Of tasseled crystal, feather, flower, fern,—
Fantastic trifles,—everywhere adorn
Its marge and sparkle in the tranquil urn;
While pendent dripstones glint and glow, and in the flickering light
Appear like Titan arms indued with harness for the fight.

XX.

Yet this is but a vestibule to halls
More gorgeous still, whose labyrinthine ways
No human foot hath traversed, on whose walls
Nor light nor eye shall linger till the days
When, following perennial snows, the rude
Autocthones shall turn where Charles's Wain
Wheels nightly 'round the pole, when men endued
With energies more potent shall attain
This altered region, frigid now, but then attuned to yield
Demeter[9] duty and afford the vineyard and the field.

XXI.

Lo! where the matron with deft hand divides
The perfumed flesh and smiling gives her lord
Choice morsels from the embers, and provides
The healthful condiment: enough reward
For her, as aye with woman, to enjoy
The secret bliss of service knit with love;
Her worship and best pleasure to employ
Her mind with cares domestic, as the dove
Delights to feed her callow brood and to the feeble nest
Devotes her constant ministry, the shelter of her breast.

[9] Demeter, goddess of agriculture.

XXII.

Judge her by this, her self-denying-soul,
All ye who speak of woman; measure not,
O man, by thine her nature nor extol
Superior sinews or profounder thought,
When these are thine, by her disparagement;
For thou art woman born and in the womb
Where thou wast fashioned her heart pulses lent
Quick motion to thy blood, and in that loom,
When first the shuttle of thy life the mystic weft began,
Her being gave response and hailed another child of man.

XXIII.

Gross is the meal, immoderate and coarse,
Their manners brutish; as they eat they cast
On either hand the refuse, fecund source,
The midden thus created, of a vast
Offensive colony of things corrupt
Which live by putrefaction and which breed
Disease and death in man or interrupt
Somatic harmony; but little heed
The cave folk give to worm or fly, contented to provide
Their daily food, theirs is the bliss to know no wish denied.

XXIV.

Deem not their lives a dull eventless round,
A joyless sequence of unvarying ways:
Their names are lost to earth, no laurel crowned
Heroic Nimrod of their race displays
His prowess in enslaving. Happy they
Whose footsteps history traceth not in war
Or legal codes or digests! Speed the day,
O Power Supreme, when no restraints shall mar
The primal freedom of thy sons save those prescribed by love,
When lion shall lie down with lamb and falcon nest with dove!

XXV.

Yet who among earth's mightiest ever dared
To rival these in deeds of high emprise?
Not he[10] who 'gainst the Cretan man-bull bared
The rock-drawn sword of Ægeus: fancy tries
In vain to picture foes more horrent than
The protoplast encountered,—hugeous bear,
Rhinoceros, and monstrous tusker,—man
The hunter then was hunted, and the lair
He called his home was only his by conquest from the dread
And fretful cave cat prowling where her spotted whelps were bred.

XXVI.

Gigantic proboscideans, mastodon,
World-wandering Nippletooth with white tusks, borne
Like Seljuk scimetars for battle drawn;
Long-fronted bisons with puissant horn;
Aurochs and urus, bear and tiger; these
He met and meeting vanquished, armed with spear
Bone-tipped and axe of silex, and the sea's
Balænic monarch churned the waves in fear
When in far Thule's shallow sounds, now high above the tide,
The patient hunter's flinty dart was buried in its side.

XXVII.

O first of world-subduers, hail, all hail!
Let loftier bards choose higher themes and sing
Of warring gods and heroes clad in mail;
Be mine the less ambitious task to bring
This humbler effort to the Muses' seat,
If haply it may move one living heart
To throb in sympathy with him whose feet
Have left no traces, albeit the part
He played on earth was nobly played, the pioneer in time
Of that immortal multitude whose footfalls are sublime.

10. Theseus.

XXVIII.

Hail, pioneer! thy struggle with the blind
Unbending forces of thine age forbade
Aught save provision for thy needs;—the mind
Advances not in states where man is made
A beast of burthen or a slave condemned
To barter liberty and life for bread.
All nature seemed thine adversary; hemmed
And girt with hostile agencies, thy thread
Of life was all too frail forsooth for thee to cultivate
The simplest arts that soften man and modify his state.

XXIX.

Perchance thou wert, as some have deemed, a child
Who lineage drew from Eden where thy sire
Leaped virile into being, undefiled
By taint hereditary; or the fire
Divine, such as Prometheus stole to give
The spark immortal to his form of clay,
Some mild arboreal satyrs, such as live
In Borneo's or Sumatra's forests, may
Have taken from His breath whose Word creative can compel
Or stocks or stones to put on life and rise His Israel.

XXX.

Whate'er thine origin, no Paradise
Knew thee as tenant, for thy lot was cast
In elemental struggle, when the ice
Slow-yielding sought the mountain snows, and vast
Mutations met thy ken while torrents bore
Alps piecemeal down, and wild confusion reigned
Where boulder-laden rivers swept the floor
Of dale and valley: thy strong soul sustained
Unflinchingly the cosmic strife although thou could'st not see
God's hand at work by drift and flood producing harmony.

XXXI.

All time is mere transition, though there be
Oppugnant eras when two periods meet,
Rereward and vanguard, on the boundary
Where each alternately prevails; the feet
Precursive of Aurora's heralds graze
The impish heels that follow in the train
Of her who sprang from Chaos, when the Day's
Glad harbingers arouse the willing swain,
And for a season rosy morn appears to linger long,
As loath to follow in the track of the anarchic throng.

XXXII.

So man, unsocial, in the pristine years,
Anarch and monarch, recognized no rule
Or limitation save his hopes and fears
As consort, sire, provider; in the school
Primæval all were children, and they learned
By instance not by precept: what are laws
But fetters on our freedom, often turned
To vilest purpose when the tyrant draws,—
Or king or mob a tyrant still,—adroitly round a land
A legal net of ordinance and tightens mesh and strand?

XXXIII.

The first of patriarchs, his sway confined
Within one little realm, was there a king
Whose loyal subjects piously enshrined
His image in their hearts: what golden ring,
Encircling conquering brows to weigh them down,
In after years, though bright with many a gem
And star-shot[11] crystal, what imperial crown
Shines with the splendour of his diadem?
His family his kingdom's bound, with simple wants and few,
He reigned supreme and tasted joys that conquerors never knew.

[11] In allusion to the opinion that the diamond is of meteoric origin.

XXXIV.

Content is happiness: that man is lord
Of all the world, whate'er may be his state,
To whom the world no pleasure can afford
Beyond his present living: though we rate
Wealth, learning, pride of place, respect of men,
As things to be desired, wanting these,—
Their lack unknown,—life may be joyous when
Sound mind and body vouchsafe perfect ease.
The untamed savage, strong in health, and blithesome as the roe,
Is happy with a bliss as pure as Fortune can bestow.

XXXV.

The lowly peasant, whistling from the plough,
Eupeptic finds his daily meal a feast
That castled lords might envy: on the brow
The sweat of agriculture plants the least
Impress of care: lie close to Nature's breast
Nor vex thy mind with theses of the schools,
Or futile explanations, leave the quest
Of'cause and essence to the learned fools
Whose puddles are their universe, so shalt thou live aright,
Each day devoted to its task, to quiet sleep the night.

XXXVI.

By nature grave, primæval man could yet
Hold sportive intercourse with his compeers;
And then as now the youths and virgins met
In simple pleasures suited to their years.
The mimic chase, where the coy virgin flees
Her ardent lover eager for the prize;
The artless dance devoid of mysteries,
But merely gladsome motion, in which eyes
Oft told a story old e'en then, but yet as new to-day
As when primæval stripling met primæval maid in play.

XXXVII.

Or round the glowing hearth the elders sat
To tell of perils mastered, of the fierce
And woolly unicorn, whose felted mat
No flint could sever and no bone could pierce;
Of cave-bear, mammoth, bison; or perchance
Some hoary senior spoke of things that live
Unseen of human eye, the sprites that dance
Within the forest glades, and those that give
Their breath to swell the tempest's roar, and those dread gnomes whose ire
Can melt the solid rock and cap the mountain snows with fire.

XXXVIII.

Or just before the gloaming, when the sun's
Last kiss had turned the summits into gold,
And night advancing summoned weary ones
To rest from toil or play, the senior told
Of Him, the great All-Father, by whose word
All things that are sprang into being, Him
Whose mandates elemental spirits heard,
And hearing did his bidding when the grim
Tongarsok,[12] lord of fire, rebelled and marshalled all the clan
Of hell-born fiends in proud revolt ere yet the world began.

XXXIX.

And oft perchance they raised their song of praise
With tongue agglutinate, link'd words with flow
Of oldest root speech, as in later days
Altaic slopes have heard or Finland's low
And swampy shores: and while their eucharist
Went up to God's high throne the sunset dyes
Of blended amber, em'rald, amethyst,
And deepest sapphire made the western skies
Seem like the portals of His heaven, a vision of the blest
Abodes where, all their trials o'er, the sons of men should rest.

(12)Tongarsok, or Torngarsuk, the Devil of the Eskimos.

XL.

Here might we leave them at the Father's feet,
The while the gates of pearl are opened wide
And swift-winged angels from the mercy seat,
Glad messengers of precious promise, glide
Gage-laden through the æther; but the Muse,
Majestic Clio, lays her strong behest,
The which no acolyte may dare refuse,
Upon the Maker[13], bidding him invest
Anew with life the valiant soul who ventured to invade,—
The first of sailors,—Neptune's realm and sought the alder's aid[14].

XLI.

Invention is but finding, and the arts
Have grown from chance disclosures and discreet
Observances of Nature, and the parts,—
Or screw or joint or arm or valve,—which meet
In some great engine stored with latent force
That infant hands might waken had their rise
Mayhap in shell or leaf, some simple source
In Nature's workshop where man's enterprise
First sought and found the types of tools by which with ready skill
He binds the elements and makes them work his sovereign will.

XLII.

Like some luxurious prodigal in haste
To pluck the specious fruit from Pleasure's tree,
So man, the great empiric, longs to taste
In every province, air and earth and sea.
With growing appetite from age to age,
Inquisitive, he hastens to explore
The mysteries of being; to assuage
His thirst for knowledge ventures from the shore
Where rev'rend custom sanctions faith, and takes each ancient creed
And makes it an episteton that he who runs may read.

---

(13) The Maker,—*i. e.*, the Poet.
(14) *Tunc alnos primum fluvii sensere cavatas.* (Virgil. Georgica. Lib. I. 136.)

XLIII.

They knew not what they sought who the remote
Well-wooded Vinland found beyond the wide
Atlantic, Lief and Biorn[15], and their boat,
Broad-beamed and buoyant, skimmed the trackless tide
Free as the albatross; their hazard urged
The later Dove [16] to take his eager flight
Where Guanahani's palmy groves emerged
To vouch his faith and glad his sailors' sight.
Thy soul was great, bold Genoese, but greater still the heart
Of thy forerunner, Lief, who knew nor astrolabe nor chart.

XLIV.

Yet who of Triton or of Viking breed
May rival him who, venturesome and brave,
Forsook the raft of osier or of reed
And launched his coracle upon the wave?[17]
An insect floating on a wrinkled leaf,
Or strip of bark upon some tranquil pool,
Or shell-housed mollusc stranded on a reef,
Perchance inspired him, though many a fool
Coeval raised the laugh of scorn, type of the fools who hurled
Their monkish gibes at him whose hand unlocked another world.

XLV.

O wayside dreamers! ye who with the eye
Of prescience see the sunrise ere the mist
And fog-banks have uplifted and descry
The Day-God's fringes! when his rays have kissed
Dome, spire and pinnacle, and when his beams
Though myth-beclouded lattice shed a flood
Of gold upon the altar stone your dreams
And ye are vindicated; martyrs' blood,
Shed at the scaffold or transformed to bitter gall by hate,
Makes fertile soil in which the thoughts of martyrs germinate.

[15]Biorn or, properly, Bjorn.
[16]Columbus.
[17]See Horace, Od. lib. I, ode iii., 9-20.

XLVI.

Like spectral ships[18] that sail against the wind
The Lord's anointed run their eager race,
Each in his generation, each assigned
His travail and his triumph, though we trace
Their course but fitfully,the constant chain
Is never broken, every age begets
Its suffering Christ-man on whom all the pain
Or sin or striving of our nature sets
The seal of expiation and for whom with cruel scorn
The world's high priests prepare the cross and plait the crown of thorn.

XLVII.

Almighty Father! can it be that Thou
Dost re-impose the burthen of this flesh
On certain of Thy children and endow
Vicarial victims with our guilt afresh?
I know not, I the Maker of this rime,
I seek not, Father, curiously to learn;
For I have sinned and suffered and my prime
Was wind-swept and afflictive.   Lo! I turn
Mine eyes to Thee, O Fount Divine, whose love retrieves the past,
Believing that to every form perfection comes at last.

XLVIII.

Thou art the source, Thou also art the end
To whom, centripetally, all things move;
In whom, when purged of all that can offend
The perfect harmony, all things behoove
To lose their special essence: when the soul,—
Mayhap through divers incarnations,—finds
A cure for will perverted and the whole
Entangling net of pride and sin which winds
Its meshes round the moral Self shall perish, then Thy Son,[19]
O God, shall climb the summits where to know and be are one.

[18]"Like spectral ships," etc.: an idea suggested, I think, by a sentence in Longfellow's "Hyperion."
[19]That is, man.

XLIX.

Like him who first adventured on the sea,
Content to rest upon its bosom, I
Confide, O Father, all my trust in Thee,
My goal and origin, nor question Thy
Divine decrees, for I too am a part,
However weak, of Thy theophany,
And in my joys and griefs and thoughts Thou art
Preparing me for that epiphany
When, this world's processes complete, Thy vivid Word shall call
All emanations to their source and God be all in all.

L.

Like drops returning to the ocean's breast
What time the labouring clouds their dews distil;
Like pilgrim swallows to their earlier nest
What time Apollo scales the northern hill
And hawthorn buds are swelling; so all life
Still upward, onward holds its steadfast way,
Each step perhaps the surer for the strife
Anterior in time, until the day
When the Erinyes[20] shall have purged the guilt from every soul
And all creation, deified, attain its final goal.

LI.

Some trunk's concavity, deprived of pith,
His galley, see the mariner afloat,
Drawn by the ebb's slow wooing through the frith
To where the sportive Nereids take his boat
Within their keeping; there on summer seas,
Kissed by the wavelet's crystal lips, we leave
Him dubious yet triumphant, while we seize
Occasion meet a coronal to weave
To decorate Poseidon's brow, if by the Muses' grace
Where amaranthine tributes hang this lay may find a place.

[20]Better known as the Furies. They are here alluded to in their truer—because older—light as purifiers.

LII.

Flow gently round my native isle to-night,
Thou steel-blue Ocean! bid thy breakers lave
Its borders lovingly where Dodman's height
Presents a reefless rampart to the wave!
May halcyon zephyrs fan thy tranquil breast
Where mild Cornubia bends her craggy horn,
Britannia's footstool planted in the west,
Where too thy murmured greeting made the morn
Of my life's day a dismal dawn with thy divining boom
Of pity as the life-star strove to pierce the gathering gloom.

LIII.

What though, a weary exile, half my span
Denied thy wholesome influence, cooped and pent
Where noisome exhalations render man
A frail and forward weakling early spent;
Where youth precocious dwindles into age
With scarce an interval of bloodless prime?
In dreams my yearning spirit bursts its cage,
And, freed by fancy, once again I climb
The coombe's green barriers, once again my eager glance is thrown
To where the Rame's brown finger points toward the Eddystone.

LIV.

And while I gaze upon thy face, O Sea!
My spirit grows akin to thine, I hold
Methinks within my hand the ready key
To England's greatness: lo! thy waves enfold
The story of her making, for thou art
Now as of yore her bulwark and her stay,
And with the throbbing of thy mighty heart
Her pulses slack and quicken day by day;
And in thine ever open page with kindling eye she reads,
As in some wizard's crystal sphere, her dauntless children's deeds.

LV.

For me once more the bold Gallants of Fowey
Sweep out from Gribben's shade with sail and oar
To curb the pride of Winchelsea or—joy
Of joys the greatest! scourge the Neustrian shore.
For me Black Philip's vultures[21] flaunt their wings
With greedy arrogance where sea and sky
Commingle, while through cove and hamlet rings
The fiery call whose echoes shall not die
While English nerves vibrate to hear in every wind that blows
How English hearts and English hands can deal with England's foes.

LVI.

But while communing thus with thee I think
But little of man's exploits, I am stirred
Like one allowed to stand upon the brink
Where life and death encounter and is heard
The sound of many waters; for, O Sea!
The finite mind beholds in thee a type
Of Highest Nature, that Immensity
Which only hath true Being; as the ripe
And perfect fruit contains within itself fruit, flower, and tree
So all earth's elements may find their counterparts in thee.

LVII.

As one who, gazing through the Tuscan's[22] glass,
Discards the guage by which men measured God
When priests were potent and the untaught mass
Took myths for verities, man's sounding rod
Explores thy chambers and his mind, enlarged,
Is meeter for creation's scope, the plan
Divine with which the universe is charged,
To manifest His glory who in man
Is seen incarnate and for whom the stars whose glittering rays
Gleam nightly on thy breast perform their canticle of praise.

[21] The Armada.
[22] Galileo.

LVIII.

The meteor dust of ages strews thy floor;
Proplasmic matter cleaves unto thy bed;
Thy teeming billows break on every shore
With life redundant; in thy depths are bred
A myriad forms thou hast not yet revealed
To man's inquiring eye; thy waters hold
Vast treasure chambers never yet unsealed,
A thousand cryptic marvels never told,
And innermost recesses where the great sea serpent glides,
Sole relic of a time when no obstruction met thy tides.

LIX.

Thy limpid shadows sparkle with the light
Of all Golconda's iridescent gems;
Thy heaving bosom trembles with its bright
Prolific phosphorescence; anadems
Of living brilliants decorate thy brows;
Thy locks are lustrous where the Nereids play;
And Nature's thaumaturgic hand endows
The dweller in thy deepest caves, where day
Can find no entrance, with their own mysterious effluence, proof
That from no creature, great or small, God's kindness stands aloof.

LX.

They called thee better than they knew of old
Who named thee Ocean, for thy waters flow
Like mighty rivers and thy streams enfold
The earth, diffusing blessings as they go
Westward surcharged with healing warmth or when,
Replete with vigour, sweeping from the poles;
The tropic breezes kiss thy lips and then
Renew their energy, like strengthened souls
Who drain the welcome goblet on some well-fought field where they
Have swung the sword for liberty throughout the livelong day.

LXI.

I love thee, Ocean, for thou art the bed
Whereon from youth to age my sires have slept
Lulled by thy melodies, and Freedom's head
Is pillowed on thy bosom; thou hast kept
Her home inviolate, the seagirt isle
Whose hills are altars where her sacred flame
Burns brightly and shall wax in splendour while
Its jealous wardens, mindful of the fame
Of those who in the days of old were nourished on thy breast,
Shall brook no rival on the wave, the realm they love the best.

LXII.

And by thine ever-sounding shore, O Sea!
Sleep those whom I have loved and loving lost:
Within the chambers of my memory
Their voices blend with thine, and I accost
Their shadows in the gloaming, when the bridge
Is swung across the narrow frith which parts
The nearer Time-shore from the misty ridge
Whose unremittent influence imparts
A chill to life like that which warns the sailor that some stark
Ice-wanderer from the arctic zone is drifting near his barque.

LXIII.

They pass before me and I call their names;
I meet their glances,—some have pitying eyes,
And some reproachful; one there is whose claims
Have challenged retribution and whose cries
The Furies, hearing, answered: grant, O God!
That this my expiation may atone;
For I have yielded to Thy chastening rod
And born correction meekly; Thou hast known
The burthen of my penitence, grant, Father, that the tears
Thine eye hath seen may purge the guilt of boyhood's heedless years.

LXIV.

O loved in life! I call; O loved and lost!
Is there not one among ye to rehearse,—
If haply they see clearer who have crossed
The Hateful river,—why the father's curse
Of pride or sensuous frenzy should convey
Inherent baseness to the spotless life,
Or stamp it slave to Passion ere its day
Of quickening in the matrix, why the strife
With sins that lie in wait, the war that every soul must wage,
Anatocismic grows the more intense from age to age.

LXV.

I call in vain, they answer not; I deem
At times they are but wraiths or soulless shades,
As unsubstantial as a morning dream,
Corporeal mists that disappear as fades
The haze that greets the sunrise. Sin is hell,
Whose depths nor men nor angels can disclose,
Whose springs united form a tainted well
Incongruous with the living stream which flows
Unsullied through the universe, that runs with love replete
From God to God until the round of goodness is complete.

LXVI.

Learn this, O man! thy secret sin will breed
Like microphytes, pervading all who draw
Their origin from thee. O woman! heed
The weighty lesson, the unerring law
Which men have called Survival,—that the sum
Of each one's vices forms a heritage
Of sensuous imperfections that benumb
And blunt the soul and grow from age to age
Like some fell parasite that clings to some great forest tree,
So sin shall waste its victim's soul, and both shall cease to be.

LXVII.

O Thou whose grace hath quickened and upheld
The Maker and enabled him to bear
The breathing of the Muses and to weld
And forge the glowing numbers and declare
The story of man's nonage! with Thy name,
As spelled by mortals, I conclude this song,
Unskilled to guess if on the tide of fame
Some kindly hap may place it with the strong
And buoyant vessels that have launched upon the dangerous sea
Since English Cædmon hewed the keel for Milton's argosy.

LXVIII.

Thine influence gives an impulse to the lyre
And tunes the poet's strain in every age;
From Thee the prophet draws the sacred fire,
By Thee the sibyl reads the secret page.
Parturient Time brings forth at Thy behest
Predestined instruments to work Thy will,—
Tyrants to scourge or ransomers whose best
Anointing is affliction; these fulfil
Their function in unfolding Thee, in Thee alone they dwell;
In every child of man the world beholds Immanuel.

LXIX.

Thus far this song hath progressed; what its worth
I know not, whether further than my strength
Can hold me I have ventured and the earth
Be fated to receive me when at length
My flagging wings miscarry. This I know
And own, O Father! that Thy loving hand
And gracious eye have led me from the low
Black depths of Disappointment: lo! I stand
Resigned yet hopeful that my verse may win a modest niche
Within the precincts of the fane whose heights it cannot reach.

LXX.

Howe'er it be, the verdict will be Thine,
For Thou art Lord of Judgments, and the gale
Of public praise or censure is divine
Alike for those who soar and those who fail.
From Thee, the Uncreated, comes the gift
Creative as an influx, and the voice
That hails the singer Poet is the swift
Corroboration of Thy Spirit's choice,
Which falls as falls the thunderbolt to shun the adjusted rod,
And throws the minstrel's mantle on the limbs elect of God.

END OF BOOK I.

SONG OF THE AGES.

BOOK THE SECOND.

BOOK THE SECOND.

THE BRONZE AGE.

I.

Majestic sisters! once again I call:
Come, loftiest daughters of Mnemosyne!
From where Leibethron's silvery showers fall
And filled Pimplæa swells the symphony.
Bring but an echo of the heavenly song,
As heard by Zeus what time with solemn tread
Around his altar the melodious throng
Intone the requiem of the godlike dead,
That we, the restless sons of toil, may catch the strains sublime,
And hear man's rhythmic footfalls strike the corridors of time.

II.

As throng the locusts see they come, they come,
The earth-born Aryans[1] from their pristine plains;
Two constant streams, as if impelled by some
Inspired vision of the wide domains
Awaiting them beyond the mountain walls
Of Ural and of Taurus and the high
Snow palaces[2] where Indra has his halls
Whose æther-piercing columns prop the sky;
Or pressed perchance by Mongol hordes, *adeva* fiends who give
No sacrifices to the gods by whom the Aryas live.

III.

They come, the nation builders, frank and free,
The Xanthochroi[3], whose eyes reflect the light
Of heaven's pure vault above them as the sea
Returns the lustre of a cloudless night.
They come, the fair-skinned wanderers, with feet
That turn not back while glory points before;
Their tramp is steady, like the waves that beat
And break with muffled music on the shore.
What barriers shall impede their march, the broad-browed race with mind
Expansive as the ocean's breast whose bounds they yet shall find?

[1]Arya, born of or possessing the earth (F. Max Muller); in later Sanskrit, noble.
[2]Sanskrit *him*, snow, and *alaya*, a dwelling-place.
[3]According to Professor Huxley's fine classification of mankind.

IV.

Westward they come, each man a Cadmus; these
Shall find Europa, and the gods shall lead
Harmonia to their couches; they shall seize
And occupy for ever, and the seed
They sow shall be the dragon's teeth, red war
The harvest of their reaping; they shall sweep
The lands as with a besom, till the far
Twin isles shall know them and the mounts that keep
Their record of Alcmene's child [4], where thankful Time shall see
Their noblest issue guard the gates of the great Median Sea.

V.

Through Khyber's rocky thoroughfare shall flow
The eastward currents, till they reach the plain
Made wealthy by the sacred rivers: lo!
The land of Holy Singers [5] where the grain
Awaits the willing sickle! They shall learn
To yoke the patient oxen, by whose aid,—
With subject Sudra service,—they shall turn
The rich alluvium, exercise repaid
A hundred-fold by Indra's grace who pours with lavish hand
Autumnal showers from his store to bless the thirsting land.

VI.

To venture and to labour and to pray,
This was their character; their minds enthroned
In spacious tenements where ample play
Is given the faculties; their ardour toned
By sure control of reason; and their speech
Strong, flexible, and copious, such as might
Have sounded first in Paradise, as teach
Some old traditions, ere the awful night
Of sin from disobedience fell upon a shuddering world,
And Yimakhshaeta's [6] golden age was into chaos hurled.

---

[4] The Pillars of Hercules—Gibraltar.
[5] Brahmarshidesha, the region of the Punjab.
[6] Yimakhshaeta (Yima) according to the Zendavesta the first Aryan king, who
reigned in the golden age.

VII.

To venture: this their spirit shall impel
Them ever onward till their restless feet
Are planted on earth's confines and the swell
Of Ocean's uninvaded realm shall greet
Their vanguard with defiance. Glory not,
Ye trumpeters of Neptune, in their stay;
Nor ye whose bridled fury fills the grot
Of Æolus with murmurs; lo! the day
Shall be when Neptune's self shall lift his placid head to see
Without rebuke their offspring share the empire of the sea.

VIII.

To labour: even in their pristine home
'Tween Oxus and Jaxartes,—names no more
Remembered by the mongrel tribes that roam
The steppes,—the furnace fused the stubborn ore
And smiths first hammered metal; here the arts
Found crude but healthy nurture, here were born
The men of skill whose history imparts
To man his chief incentive; when the morn
Of the new era shall arise the theme the poet sings
Shall be the artist mind and hand instead of priests and kings.

IX.

To pray: at first to God, the One, the All,
Spirit Supreme by whom the world was made.
Thrice happy mortals could we now recall
The antique faith and be no more afraid
Of sanctuary idols! Burn thy tomes,
Theologaster, weary not the stars
With idle concepts where the fancy roams
From attribute to attribute; the bars
Are rigid as relentless fate which keep thee shut within
Thine ectoderm; restrain thy pride! to picture God is sin.

X.

Accursed craft that used the maker's myth
To work the slavery of the human mind!
That bent his subtile fancies as the smith
To make his image hammers the refined
And shining metal till he moulds a face
And figure like his own, perchance with arm
Hypertrophied with labour!   As we trace
The line to priest from poet half the charm
Is taken from the ancient lore, we drop the myths aghast,
And like some mitred clowns of old we turn iconoclast.

XI.

O ye who dwell within the classic shades
Where gentle Isis bends to meet the Thame,
Whose seal upon their unridged foreheads aids
The climbing adolescents when the flame
Of genius fails because the empty lamp
Of vulgar clay no subsidy receives!
Be watchful, lords of learning, that you stamp
No obsolescent oracle; the leaves
That autumn's finger turns to gold have had their day I ween,
No season's change may give them life, no sun recall their green.

XII.

Thames, Tiber, Seine, and Ganges! on your banks
The twice-born Aryans are being born again.
Once more the boding murmur stirs the ranks,
Once more the nations are being roused as when
Great Rudra[7] shakes the forest.   Be ye wise,
Ye Brahmans, and your caste shall haply be
Now as of yore their leaders! see ye prize
The truth where'er it lead you; though ye see
Foundations totter hasten not, for novelty deceives,
Beware lest going to Jericho ye fall among the thieves.

[7]Rudra, the Storm-god of the Rigveda.

XIII.

Away with text and commentary till
Ye learn the primer of the threefold page,—
The ever-open volume where His will
God's hand recording writes in every age.
The starry vault, the world, the human heart,—
Read these aright with unbeclouded eye
And mind unclogged with maxims; then impart
The truths ye gather freely; prophesy,
If moved, as bold interpreters, nor strive to square and trim
God's Word and Wisdom to the moulds of timeworn teraphim.

XIV.

O venerable masters! while ye pore
O'er old traditions lovingly the minds
Ye led while in their pupillage may soar
Beyond tradition, and the faith which binds
Them to finality perchance may yield
To Truth's demands, as step by step men learn
A broader scripture everywhere revealed,
Which tells that Love Ineffable doth burn
With equal brightness unto all, the Bible where we trace
Impartiality divine that knows no favoured race.

XV.

O sacred Truth, thou sun of all the spheres!
Break through the clouds of Eld, direct thy bright
And piercing radiance where the dust of years
In hall and quadrangle obscures the light.
Bid eye meet eye in candour; bid the weak
Be strong to spurn the fetters that corrode
And dwarf the intellect; bid Reason speak
Through lips that long have faltered; lift the load
Of paltry compromise, O Truth! that gown and hood may be
The symbols of a fellowship whose roots are laid in thee.

XVI.

O Thou Mysterious One whose name I use
What time on bended knee I urge my soul
To converse with its Origin! excuse
The feeble faith that asks Thee to console
Yet lacks assurance.   Through the mists of time
The oracles show dimly, and we hear
Thy gentle voice in echoes; thy sublime
Surrender and oblation call the tear
To eyes that, like the Sadducees', with haughty scorn repel
Thy claim to be the Christ of God, the Hope of Israel.

XVII.

True Man and Brother! in my utmost need,
When surging billows break above my head,
When blasts from Tophet sway me as the reed
Is bent before the whirlwind, be my stead!
O'er the broad gulf of centuries Thy hand,
Marked with the stigma of the worldling's hate,
Traces once more the scripture in the sand,
And points the wanderer to the mercy-gate.
Be this to me Thy gospel, Lord, the promise fixed and sure:
"Neither do I condemn thee child; depart and sin no more!"

XVIII.

What pen, O Clio, wrote the fateful word
Which time confirming turned to prophecy?
What ear of man so favoured that it heard
The promise of the future, the decree
That Japheth's bounds should be enlarged, the tents
Of Shem become his dwelling[8]?   Gracious Muse,
Restore for me the crumbled battlements
Of old Confusion's tower, let me use
That coign of vantage while I gaze on Shinar's plain and trace
With fancy's eye the babbling source of nation, tribe, and race.

---

[8]"God shall enlarge Japheth, and he shall dwell in the tents of Shem: and
Canaan shall be his servant."   Genesis IX. 27.

XIX.

The wavering clouds are parted, and a breeze
From steep Niphates sweeps the affluent plain;
The doubt-mists scatter and the dreamer sees
The hopeless builders abdicate the vain
And futile enterprise: the childish lore,
The legends gathered at a mother's knee
From quaintest pencillings revive once more,
And with them half the ancient faith,—I see
Birs Nimrod's winding causeway, note each worker strive to reach
Some sympathetic group to claim the brotherhood of speech.

XX.

Reluctantly, with many a fond regret
Lo! Mizraim's clans begin their pilgrimage
To Khem's far distant valley; they shall set
Their roots below the surface, and the page
Of human history shall be theirs till time
Has tried and found them wanting, yet their day
Shall be full glorious and their sun shall climb
To high meridian splendour, their decay
Shall last while empires wax and wane, and cause Oblivion's head[9]
To turn in wonder to the Sphinx as though old Time were dead.

XXI.

Unwilling nomads, God shall guide their feet
O'er mount and plain until their eager eyes
Shall see, beyond the narrow bridge where meet
Two continents, the mystic river rise.
There shall they find, on Khem's black soil, a home,
A fertile land, a land of brick and stone,
Concordant with their genius; and each nome
Shall be a human anthill, there alone
Shall man presume to cope with fate and raise with cunning hand
Enduring monuments to brave the whirlwind and the sand.

---

[9] "Time sadly overcometh all things, and is now dominant and sitteth upon a sphinx, and looketh unto Memphis and old Thebes, while his sister Oblivion reclineth semi-somnous on a pyramid, gloriously triumphing, making puzzles of Titanian erections, and turning old glories into dreams." (Sir Thomas Browne.)

XXII.

Vain hope! the death he dreaded Mizraim could
Nor curb nor conquer; even at his board
His mirth was overcast, the spectre stood
Between him and the winecup; as he poured
The red juice from the flagon effigies
Arrayed in cerecloths met his daunted eye,
While hollow voices thundered, "Look on these!
Eat, drink, be merry, for thou too must die!"[10]
Build, Mizraim, mansions for the dead,—the fruit of all thy toil
Shall be when peasant hands shall strew thy dust on foreign soil.[11]

XXIII.

The patriarch's curse that fell on Canaan's head
Ere yet his thews were hardened fell on thee.
O Mizraim his brother! thou wast dead
In spirit, sunk in foul idolatry
While in thy pride of place the world was thine.
Corruption seized thee, and thy carious limbs
Were plunged in putrefaction as the swine
Roll grovelling in the mire, and the whims
And filthy fancies of thine heart thy children deified
Until thy very leprosy was sacro-sanctified.

XXIV.

Pubescent purity, that stood amazed
At Nature's revelation, lost its blush
Of conscious chastity, thy hand erased
The bloom of innocence as one might crush
A rosebud ere it opened; and thy gods
Were misbegotten monsters,—strange that we,
Earth's later children, cherish still the frauds
The Nile mud fostered, make the blasphemy
Of God-resisting Typhon serve as manacles to bind
The limbs of Progress and prolong the slavery of the mind!

[10]Herodotus, "Euterpe," 78. A somewhat ghastly provocative to good fellowship and an extreme insistence on the maxim, *Ede, bibe, lude, nulla est in morte voluptas.*
[11] Shiploads of mummies have been brought from Egypt and used as fertilizers in Europe.

XXV.

Mayhap the amercement of thy father's sin
Of guilty seeing fell on thee; no glimpse
Of Love Ineffable might fall within
Thine opaque vision blinded by the imps
And slime of Tophet.   By thy conscious fears
The nations have been tainted: life for life,[12]—
Dark dogma of damnation! all the years
Of man's abandonment of God are rife
With Substitution's sighs and tears: accursed creed! thy dread
Persuading wove the crown of thorns that pierced the Sinless Head!

XXVI.

Through time's dark caverns still the echoes roll
Of David's bitter protest, of the cry
That rose to heaven from his anguished soul:
"Lord, I have sinned! why should my people die?"
The scapegoat's bones have whitened in the sand
And turned to dust with them whose sins it bore
Into the wilderness, and Mizraim's hand
Hath long since lost its cunning, yet we pour
The vials of the wrath of God on Calvary's Crucified,
And make His tender shoulders bear the burthen of our pride.

XXVII.

Creative Essence, whose high attributes
Defy our finite standards, may Thy grace
Condone the impious fiction that imputes
To Thee our motives! dissipate the base
And baneful doctrines by which men conceive
Thee as a cruel Apis-dæmon urged
To salve thine own prerogatives; relieve
The human mind, through ages whipped and scourged
By its own bugbears; spread Thy light, that all mankind may see
Man needs no scapegoat, God of Love, to make him one with Thee!

---

[12] Herodotus, "Euterpe," 39; compare Leviticus, XVI. 21, 22, for a borrowed
rite. For a more rational and humane belief see Micah, VI. 7, 8,—"Shall I give
my firstborn, etc.?"

XXVIII.

In all incarnate let Thy Word and Life,—
True Son and Spirit,—dwell with us and lift
Our souls to higher levels; bid the strife
Of dubious oracles to cease; the gift
Of honest speech impart to all who bear
The message of Thy Fatherhood, that they
Soil not their souls with sophistry nor wear
The vestments of the Pharisee; repay
The blood of all Thy martyrs, Lord, may every drop they shed
In patient witness fall in streams of kindness on our head!

XXIX.

Enlighten Thou our reason, purge the dross
That dulls the intellect, that so man's thought
May rise above all partial views and cross
The Alps that thwart our vision! cancel aught
That tends to idol worship, love of self,
Indulgence, daintiness, and lust of praise;
To nobler issues than the race for pelf
Inspire our children to devote their days!
As Thou Thyself art One, O God, the primal, perfect Good,
Bid poet, priest, and craftsman join in kindly brotherhood!

XXX.

'Twas thus, O Mizraim, that thy day was spent,
The earth was thine and thou wast of the earth;
Thy children served the fleshpots and they bent
Their backs to carnal burthens; from thy birth
Thy heart was brutish and thy genius turned
To subterranean idols, thou didst sit
By thine own choice while yet thy taper burned
In fullest splendour by the awful pit[13]
Whose sides are lined with sepulchres, the graves where nations fell
Who sought like thee their paradise within the womb of hell.

[13]Ezekiel, XXXII. 23.

XXXI.

Egypt! the nurse of letters and of law,
Where social order, stated government,
And commerce had their origin; that saw
The arts instructive gain development!
Thy relics are a Bible where we read,
As day by day unrolls its palimpsest,
The causes of thy ruin,—thou didst lead
Thyself to thy undoing when the pest
Of priestly usurpation passed unheeded through the land
And Superstition's loathsome brood upheld the tyrant's hand.

XXXII.

Thou gav'st us gods, O Egypt, but the spark,
The vital spark, of liberty ne'er shone
Upon their altars, and the holy ark
Of Freedom came not nigh thee, thou alone
Didst disregard the tree whose roots have crept
Adown the mountains, and whose leaves are stored
With healing for the nations who have kept
Their hearts untainted; and the sacred sword
That patriot freemen love to draw was never forged in thee,
Where twice ten thousand cities slept in servile lethargy.

XXXIII.

Two warring elements benumbed thy soul,—
The negro's passion and the Shemite's gloom;
The he-goat's promptings nothing could control,
Corruption's terrors drove thee to the tomb.
Conquered and conquering by turns, thy blood
Has mingled with the Nile's black ooze and spread
A crimson mantle o'er the mystic flood,
As when Jehovah's foundling gave the dread
Foretoken to the tyrant, when the smitten waters bore
Through Pathros and through Mazor's plain the putrefying gore.

XXXIV.

All nations met within thy gates,—thy peer
In art and arms, great Asshur, and thy wise
Chaldæan congener, with those that steer
Their ships to Tarshish and the land that lies
Fast anchored in the ocean: when the tooth
Of time hath marred thy beauty, then, O Khem!
In that far isle shall man renew his youth
And speak of thee as of a thrice-told dream.
Rock tomb and pyramid and sphinx shall tell their tale to these,
And Hebrew pilgrims stand amazed before dead Rameses.[14]

XXXV.

The lapidary's symbols still abide,
Enduring censors of humanity:
Birs Nimrod's ruins chasten human pride,
The pyramids rebuke our vanity.
O cares of men [15], frivolity of kings!
A granite mountain could not guard the bones
Of haughty Khufu, and oppression brings
Its condemnation; lo! the toilers' groans,
The sighs, the sweat, the sullenness of outraged manhood call
To God for justice till the hands of retribution fall.

XXXVI.

It is the curse of power that it tends
To exaltation, Pharaohs, Cæsars feed
With flatteries their frailties; Heaven sends
No blessing when it gluts the miser's greed.
The anointed tyrant deems his right divine,
His cringing courtiers bend as to a god;
Sleek Dives struts through factory or mine,
While toilworn wagelings tremble at his nod.
Unskilled to keep the golden mean, huckster and king deride
The patient shoulders that support their luxury and pride.

---

[14] Rameses II. His mummy was unwrapped by Maspero, June 1, 1886.
[15] *O curas hominum! O quantum est in rebus inane!* (Persius.)

XXXVII.

O Christ, Thou Carpenter of Nazareth!
Inspire Thy ministers that they may live
Thy life of self-denial! then Thy death
Shall prove man's resurrection and shall give
A crown to Labour! kindle in their breasts
The ardour of Thy sympathy and break
Asunder custom's shackles! hurl the tests
And caste-marks to oblivion! bid them make
Their Master their Exemplar that in very deed the world
May see the banner of man's rights by priestly hands unfurled!

XXXVIII.

Gethsemane, the mount, the sepulchre,
All these we know; in homily and hymn
The tears, the tree, the cerements all recur,
But not the humble workshop with its grim
Diurnal tragedy of sordid toil,
Bent back and stiffened muscles, grimy hand
And calloused fingers,—too uncouth a foil
For chasuble and mitre! Lo! they stand,
The frank and sturdy labourers ye fain would win, outside
The fanes where Christians emphasize their luxury and pride!

XXXIX.

Hail, glorious day when adventitious gauds
From loom and needle stand no more as signs
Of worth in man or woman, when the odds
Of rank or fortune mark no more the lines
Of social merit! Priest and poet then,
Untrammelled by forged fetters, shall conspire
To animate and bless the sons of men;
The voice of Nature speaking through the lyre
Shall call to Pisgah's heights while they who serve the altar stand
To consecrate the hosts that march toward the Promised Land.

XL.

Phœnicia, home of commerce! by the oath
Thy grandson[16] swore to Philip I invoke
The heavenly sisters halting as if loath
To light upon thy seaboard, for the yoke
The trafficker bears lightly is a clog
To higher impulse, and the art divine
But seldom sends its search-light through the fog
That followed thine eclipse; the Philistine,
Thy gallant neighbour, Israel's scourge, has left a loftier name,
His warworn buckler rightly hangs in the bright halls of fame.

XLI.

By Sun and Moon, Earth, Mead, and River! by
Thine own great highway, the historic Sea!
I exorcise thy genius and descry
The sister cities with their galaxy
Of banked and beaked sea-castles, quinquereme
And argosy, equipped alike for war
And commerce, and I note the steady stream
That brings the wealth of Sheba and the far
Peninsula, the caravans whose fragrant freight shall rise
Where sacrificial censers swing in incense to the skies.

XLII.

Lo! hive-like Tyre issues from the flood,
As rose Ashtarte in her blushing shell.
A thousand caldrons hold the purple blood
Of the pressed mollusc, street and factory tell
Of industry and fullness; wealth waxed fat[17]
And reared its garners higher than the walls
Of royal palaces, while Mammon sat
With luxury and lewdness in her halls.
And dark-eyed captives from the Isles of Tin in wonder stood
To see Ashtarte's priests exact the tithe of maidenhood.

[16] Hannibal the Carthaginian: Polybius, VII. 2, 9.
[17] Ὄλβος ἄγαν παχνθείς.

XLIII.

From Calpe's Strait to Cyprian Salamis
The wheeling seagulls flap their ceaseless wings
In concert with the oar-blades as they kiss
Their mirrored shadows, while the prorate[136] sings
His matin hymn to Baal as they sweep,
Proud argosies rich-freighted, past each ness
And castled headland where the wardens keep
Their constant seawatch; and the rowers press
In eager rivalry to win the prize they most desire,
And claim the fleet's pre-eminence for Sidon or for Tyre.

XLIV.

Bright sea, whereto the world's great empires came
And laved their feet through ages! who shall say
What changes yet await thee, who shall claim
Thy lordship when the clouds have passed away
Which gather now about thee? Haply fate
May hold in store some pebble that shall smite
The dread colossus even as the great
Goliath sunk sore smitten when the white
Brook boulder fell, or as the huge dream-image was o'erthrown
Whose feet incongruous turned to dust beneath the unhewn stone.

XLV.

The tyrant's hands, that shiver while they hold
The rod of empire on the Neva's banks,
May seize Byzantium and the Horn of Gold,
While Slav and Finn and Kalmuck dress their ranks
On either side Propontis. Then, great sea,
The Romanoff shall dip his knout and chains
In thy blue waters, but they shall not free
Or thong or fetter from the shameful stains
Of outraged Poland's noblest blood; parturient time shall bring
The Slav himself to Freedom's shrine to hear the joy bells ring.

[136] προράτης, or προρεύς, the lookout on the forecastle.

XLVI.

Build up, ye silent workers of the deep,
A rosy rampart! suffer, too, thy bed,
O sea, to lift its bosom that the steep
Primæval causeway may appear that led
Huge Libyan mammals to the hither shore,—
The river-horse and that great tusker whose
Effodial relics wondering peasants tore
With straining spade and mattock from the ooze
Of old Helorus,—burst, ye fires of Vulcan, burst in glee
When Freedom's offspring prove too weak to keep the Midland Sea!

XLVII.

Thou hast the keys, Britannia, in thy hand;
The lion rock of Tarik, it is thine:
And on Valetta's knightly towers stand
The emblems of thine empire.   Lo! the sign
Of man's redemption, battletorn yet bright,
St. George's cross, flies bravely in the breeze!
Look well, Britannia, that no foreign wight
Remove the standard or assume the keys.
Let Rooke and Clayton's, Eliott's fame inspire thy soul to guard
The azure, sun-kissed thoroughfare of which thou art the ward!

XLVIII.

Phœnicia in her noonday prime begat
A greater daughter, Carthage, and her feet
She planted where the queenly Dido sat
With royal state in Juno's porch to greet
The wandering Trojan,—lo! the Lovely One,
Erato, comes unbidden, and the twain,
Her statelier sisters, smile in unison
Their hesitating welcome, as if fain
To spare their votary's tender breast, for well they ken that he
Who gazes on Erato's charms transfers his loyalty.

XLIX.

With gentle voice that like a limpid brook
Glides smoothly on she weaves her subtle spell.
I see once more the Tyrian sisters look
To where the ready galleys meet the swell.
The unbrailed sail hangs loosely, at the stern
I note the pilgrim father, in his ear
The cry of duty echoes; Love may burn
In vain his perfumed torches, when that clear
Alarm rings o'er the bounding sea, though lulled in Beauty's arms,
The true man always wakes and sets his face against her charms.

L.

O Lovely One! though time's auturgic loom
Has scattered threads of silver o'er his head,
His heart will throb susceptive till the tomb
Shall ope its portals to the poet dead!
The Mantuan Master saw with equal eye
And even pulses,—spare thou me, O Muse!
Who looks within thy crystal globe may die
With bootless longing, yet who may refuse
Such divination at thy call, thou loveliest of the Nine,
And hope to win the threshold where the lute is held divine?

LI.

A marble chamber opening to the sea
Through lofty arches; from the capitals
Of slender columns hangs a canopy
Of gold embroidered purple; on the walls
The maidens weep for Adon. All that Tyre
Can show of skillful workmanship is here;
Pride, wealth, love, luxury, and art conspire
To grace the haunt Elisa holds most dear.
For this is Dido's solitude where first she learned to trace
And read the signs of ripening love in the great wanderer's face.

LII.

A golden tripod stands beside her couch
Of purple-pillowed cedar,—yestereve
An altar where two loving hearts did vouch
A faith whose fervour nothing could bereave.
Filled flagon, goblet, philtre, many a sweet
Provocative to pleasure,—now, alas!
The mute remembrancers of him whose feet
With welcome music never more shall pass
Within the threshold of this shrine, of him whose voice could thrill
The widowed breast, whose glance subdue a queen's imperious will.

LIII.

The evening star gleams like a crystal tear
Upon the cheek of Beauty in the west;
Ashtarte's silver crescent follows near,
Like some lone galley lighted to its rest.
Their blended radiance falls on her who kneels
Within the marble chamber and whose eyes
In anguish turn where every eye appeals
Since the first sufferer vainly sought the skies.
Could mortal loveliness prevail to turn the tide of fate,
Deserted Dido, thou would'st not be thus disconsolate!

LIV.

Her raven tresses stream all unconfined,
Save for an azure fillet edged with gold,
Below her swelling flexures as the wind
Trails the black storm-cloud o'er the snowy wold.
Her veil of gossamer neglected clings,—
A cobweb dew-besprinkled,—just beneath
Her heaving breast's twin cupolas and flings
Athwart her glowing loveliness a wreath
Diaphanous as morning rime whose glittering crystals bear
Augmented greenness to the mead and perfume to the air.

LV.

One hand is raised imploringly, as though
To claim an instant succour from the mild,
Chaste love-star's eye that sees her secret woe;
The other held as if to still the wild
Commotion in her bosom; on her limbs,
Whose tapering fullness prompts to worship, hinge
Two gleaming anklets, but their lustre dims
Beside the living marble's rosy tinge.
O recreant one! return and find a kingdom to thy hand
Whose present bliss may well requite the lapsed Lavinian land!

LVI.

He comes not back: O breaking heart be still!
While time endures woman shall endure
The grief that knows no anodyne until
Death's soothing fingers work the perfect cure.
Unhappy Dido! in that white-cliffed isle,
Whereto thy subjects ply the labouring oar,
A fairer Helen[19] than the one whose smile
Beguiled the faithless Dardan shall deplore
In coming years the cruel fate that leaves the rustic free
To live and love while princes bear a burthen none may see.

LVII.

Through dusky cloisters of the Past the low
And solemn strains of human sorrow glide,
Like some great organ sounding sweet and slow
Through nave and transept at the eventide.
The dirge of love that stood beside the grave
Of its own happiness and hid the tear;
Of hopes that had no fruitage, joys that gave
A moment's glow and perished; of the sere
And withered friendships that have turned to dust when fortune fled,—
The endless coronach that time sits crooning o'er the dead.

[19]*Quo, Musa, tendis?*
"The object, and the pleasure of mine eye,
Is only Helena. To her, my lord,
Was I betroth'd ere I saw Hermia."
Let no profane hand disinter the secret (hidden in the text) of two royal hearts,
one of which shall beat no more for ever.

CARMEN MORTALE.

Warrior! sheathe thy dinted sword,
   Lay thy buckler down.
'Gainst the fierce invading horde
Thou thy blood hast freely poured,—
   Claim the victor's crown!
Cross thy hands upon thy breast,
Shut thine eyes and take thy rest!

Pilot! strike thy tattered sail,
   Make thy moorings fast.
Nor rocks to lee nor gulf nor gale
Shall cause thy rugged cheek to pale,
   Now thy voyage is past,
Safe upon the eternal shore,
Time and tide shall vex no more!

Mother! lay that golden head
   Gently on its bier.
Could thy grief recall the dead,
Would'st thou venture then to shed
   One disturbing tear?
Weep not for the lambs that dwell
In the meads of asphodel!

Maiden! twine thy wreath anew:
   Lo! the orange bloom
Wilting frost hath fingered, rue,
Cypress, and the poisoned yew
   Best beseem the tomb.
Dream not of thy lover's vows,
Death hath claimed thee for his spouse!

    *   *   *

Open thy breast, sweet mother!
 Earth, open wide thy breast
When the night shall fall and another
 Of thy nurslings sink to rest,
To awake on the glad to-morrow,
 When the Sun of Suns shall rise
On eyes that have seen thy sorrow,
 Ears that have heard thy cries!

LVIII.

The wooded crest of Gilead's wall is stirred
By seaborn zephyrs ready to expire;
I hear the lowing of a mighty herd
Whose hoofs have churned the Jabbok ford to mire.
Beyond the brook's perennial flow I spy
A halting pilgrim; as his heavy feet
Approach the shelving watershed the sky
O'er Ammon's waste is lightened, and I greet
With fancy's eye the Prince of God, whose seed like him shall strive
Throughout oppression's longest night and wrestling shall survive.

LIX.

Castanean-eyed, with visage like the keen
Sea-eagle brooding on some beetling cliff,
Lo! Jacob the Supplanter! in his mien
See resolution mixed with care, as if
He doubted Esau's welcome.   Well he knows
That here glib tongue and ready wit may fail;
The cozener's craft is feebleness when foes
Foregather in the desert; what avail
The musty cobwebs men term laws, pandects and pundits when
Their victims seize the sword and call their birthright back again?

LX.

Shepherd and goatherd, go thy way in peace!
Thy brother will not harm thee; thou and he
Are types whose counteraction shall not cease
While man the unit deems his gain can be
A righteous spur and sanction. Noble souls
There shall be in all ages, Esaus who
Shall scorn the sordid publican whose tolls
Are sweat begrimed and bloody: these, the few,
Shall be the leaven that shall work till the whole lump shall rise
With ordered energy and share an equal enterprise.

LXI.

'Tis thine, O Wrestler! thine to strive with God
And make of Him thy partner, lulled in sleep
While all things answer to thy hope; the rod
Of great Jehovah's anger thou shalt keep
Abeyant to thy purpose; when thy life
Hangs wavering in the balance and the fell
Floods lift their voice against thee, lo! the strife
Shall then be holy, God and Israel
Shall smite the tents of Amalek, of Ammon, Gebal, Tyre,
And make them like a potter's wheel or wood before the fire.[20]

LXII.

Jehovah! By the magic of that name
A nomad horde shall win a place among
The commonwealth of nations and the flame
Of unity be nourished and the tongue
Of lisping infants in all lands shall tell
His praises and a subject world shall sing
The songs first heard in Zion;—how they swell,
Those lyric offerings of the poet king,
Above the wailing of the world, those sacred strains that blend
The God of Kadesh with the One whose mercies have no end!

[20] Psalm LXXXIII. 13, 14.

LXIII.

Be this thy glory, Israel, that thou
Didst raise thy tribal deity by slow
And toilsome stages to the mountain's brow
Where pure Isaiah felt the vivid glow
Of Light Ineffable, the flash that shone
On that lone prophet by the Zuyder Zee
With fuller radiance and revealed the throne
Of Him whose name and being are To Be!
Be this thy glory, Israel, thou learned'st to read aright
The sacred tetragrammaton, Substance, Word, Wisdom, Light!

LXIV.

And we, the heirs of time, for whom the earth
Shall don dædalian beauties when the sun
Of the new golden age shall bring to birth
Fresh forms and forces,—when we too have won
The Pisgah heights and view with eager eyes
The summer-land our portion stretching broad
Beyond our vision, we shall recognise
With thankful hearts the sacred hill where God
Preserved the consecrated flame to light the welkin when
United faith and science shed their unveiled beams on men.

LXV.

O harp of Zion! while the world shall last
Thy heavenly melody shall strike the ear
Beyond all other music and shall cast
Its wondrous gifts of healing far and near.
Solace and hope and impulse, this shall be
The prelude to the universal song
Of men and angels through eternity,
Of slaves made free, of feeble souls made strong.
The isles shall hear the strains sublime when Israel's house shall fail
And Jacob's seed shall scattered be like chaff before the gale.

LXVI.

O Lord of Life! O Quickening Spirit! Thou
First Emanation from the Uncreate!
Divine Hypostasis who dost endow
All things distinctive that may demonstrate
The God in Process! with a poet's zeal
I laud and magnify Thy glorious name[2]
In grateful rapture that Thou didst reveal
The Father first to poets and proclaim
In artless hymns transcending art His mercy and His might
From whom all things proceed, the goal in whom all things unite!

LXVII.

Inspired by Thee, O Lord of Life! the tones
Of Zion's harp sound resonant and clear,
And rise above the valley of dry bones
Where outcast Israel sheds the exile's tear.
As in Kaffraria's loam the delver brings
To light some brilliant for a monarch's crest
Or as the phœnix preens her golden wings
In desert sands and builds her fragrant nest
Where none may see her sacrifice, so through the awful gloom
Of wayward Israel's guilt and fall that harp adorns his tomb.

LXVIII.

Can these bones live? Degraded, sordid, cold,
The Gentile's parasite and eke his scorn,
Sweeping his market while they clip his gold,
Can these bones live and Jewry rise new-born?
Lip-loyal to all princes, true to none;
Gath'ring in fields where other men have strowed
The seeds of peace and progress; quick to shun
With alien craft the sacred duty owed
By freemen when their country calls; can such revive to dwell
Where David's thirty stood to guard the mount of Israel?

---

[2] See the Communion Service,—the Preface. "Therefore with Angels, etc."

LXIX.

Can these bones live? Yes, when from Jacob's stock
One shoot shall rise whose manly heart shall be
Warm with ancestral energies to mock
The recreant maxim of the Sadducee[22]
That Israel hath no waking.   Then the voice
The prophet heard by Chebar shall proclaim
A people's resurrection to rejoice
The house so long left mourning and reclaim
Her barren wastes, rebuild her walls, and raise on Zion's height
A nobler temple wherein Jew and Gentile shall unite.

LXX.

Unite in highest worship at the shrine
Of that great Fatherhood where all are priests
To dedicate the bread and bless the wine,
And bid the nations to the solemn feasts.
Speed Thou the day, O Quickener! when the Jew
Shall light the torch of liberty and stand,
No mercenary warrior, with the true
Knights banneret who hold with steady hand
Aloft the standard of our rights, the labarum to lead
The army of man's social hope to vanquish crime and greed!

LXXI.

Steed of the Morning! fold thy strenuous wings.
And gently light on yonder peak whose grey
And furrowed forehead from the cloud-belt springs
Like some steep islet wreathed in ocean's spray!
Lightly descend, O Pegasus! and see
Thy mien be tractable; strike not thy hoof
To force forbidden fountains; suffer me.
A timorous trespasser, to stand aloof
From thee Medusa-sprung! and muse; for this alone I dare
To stand upon Parnassus hill and breathe its hallowed air.

[22]"To shame the doctrine of the Sadducee."   Byron, *Childe Harold.*

LXXII.

As in some Thracian gardens where the rose
O'ertasks the gale with fragrance, every wind
Comes incense-laden hitherward and blows
Ambrosial burthens to oppress the mind.
The marshall'd memories cluster o'er my head
And baffle distribution, and I hear
A murmur like the voices of the dead
Which Dreamland zephyrs bring to mortal ear.
"Bend low," they whisper, "child of earth, upon the altar floor
Where Genius comes to sacrifice from every clime and shore!"

LXXIII.

Oh! might I reach to such high meed that I
Were numbered with the acolytes to stand
A server at that altar ere I die
And wear the vestments of that radiant band!
To know that as the swelling chorus swept
From age to age one note of mine would last,—
What then were exile or the tears long wept
For love vows broken and for friendships past?
Though sterile life's meridian hour, the gloaming Oh! how sweet,
Dear Land of Refuge! could I lay one laurel at thy feet!

LXXIV.

O Thou whose purpose passes human thought
Save that it calls man to renounce, or yield
His hopes at their fruition! Thou hast taught
My spirit acquiescence and hast steeled
My breast to disappointment, and I bear
The ordeal meekly even as I hide
The dart whose lesion nothing can repair,
Or press the thorn Thou gavest to my side.
One fluttering hope I still have kept, one feeble, glimmering ray
Has pierced the world's disdain and cheered my solitary way.

LXXV.

For this I brave the Loxian's wrath and set
My faltering feet where earth's Immortals trod;
Though vain the vision, end it not nor yet
Dispel the dream or quench the hope, O God!
Vain though it be, it is my all, I gave
To one fond wish the worship of long years,
Man's friendship, love of woman,—let the grave
That hides the dreamer hide the dreamer's tears!
While life remains permit the thought that haply Fame may give
One modest nook within her halls where this my song may live!

LXXVI.

Here, from Parnassus, once again I spy
The world-inheritors, earth-born, whose course
Is on the necks of nations; from the high
And many-ridged Olympus to the source
Of old Eurotas, mount and vale and plain
Confess the title of their leaf-shaped brands
And spears of tempered metal, where the stain
Impairs the lustre of the bronze and stands
A silent witness to the might of Hellen's sons who bore
Unwittingly from kindred hands the notched Pelasgian shore.

LXXVII.

On well-walled Tiryns' rocky height the eyes
Of young Alcides turn toward the sea,
While nereids whisper of the isle that lies
Beyond Cythera, where Pasiphae
Taught Art to outrage Nature. Everywhere
The soil breeds heroes and the seed is set
Whose shoots expanding to the sun shall bear
Such fruitage as Igdrasil never yet
Put forth in bud or fragrant bloom, the tree of life shall rise
Like some great eucalypt until its crown shall reach the skies.

LXXVIII.

Wide, bold, and free as morning gales that sing
When rosy Eos hails the Cyclades,
Exultant manhood bends its thews to spring
As some young athlete bows his limber knees
Before the threshold[23] when the stadium waits
The signal for the running, or as when
The wrestler crouches and anticipates
The grip on thigh or buttock: these the men
Of Hellas in her mewing youth in whom with added worth
The pristine Aryan soul attains another, kindlier birth.

LXXIX.

A kindlier birth, because their deeds were sung
By those whose strains were potent as the lyre
Of Orpheus when the gates of Hades swung
And softened Pluto granted his desire.
Not mine, O Muse! to emulate their songs
With tongue less flexile and with soul less free;
Be mine the modest motive that belongs
To humbler themes and minor minstrelsy;
Therewith content, so may I rove on Helicon and fill
My heart with music from the myths that haunt the muses' hill!

LXXX.

That music still can charm the strictest ear
Beyond all other melody! as when
The shepherd boy of Ascra[24] caught the clear
Melodious whispers of his native glen.
Breathings divine that all unbidden spring
From wood and stream and the blue sky above;
The voice of Nature bidding poets sing,
The Voice Creative bidding mortals love.
Divinest harmonies like those Ayr's gentle songster stole
From the brown lavrock's nest to cheer the durance of his soul.

---

[23] Threshold, *i.e.*, the stone bar which formed the starting-point in the footrace.
At Olympia "the starting-point and the goal in the Stadion were marked by lime-
stone thresholds." (Prof. Jebb in Encyc. Brit.)
[24] The poet Hesiod.

LXXXI.

From birth till death enswathed in falsehood, we
Know not the joy of living, every lie
We cherish adds its quota to the sea
Whose ebon waves reflected foul the sky.
Lies of the school, the forum, and the mart,
The juggling sophistry of those who steer
The ship of Progress by an antique chart,
And hug the quicksands in unmanly fear
Of that wide ocean tempting man to search its breast and seize
With hero-soul the isles of hope, the new Hesperides.

LXXXII.

Not thus thy children, Hellas, in thy youth;
Their red blood danced with vigour and they saw
With childlike singleness of eye the truth
That human happiness is Heaven's law.
They joyed in living, from the ample store
Of their vitality they peopled earth,—
The stream, the forest, and the sounding shore,—
With forms of richest fancy, at whose birth
The muses were the midwives who first taught the bard to sing
And ordered that in fancy's realm the poet should be king.

LXXXIII.

And from the treasure chamber of his mind
The poet chose appellatives and named
The bright creations, and to each assigned
His place and function; thus compactly framed
There rose the pantheon; the goodly halls
Whose mazy courts the diligent may tread
And solve the riddles of the sculptured walls,
And learn the deathless wisdom of the dead,
The fables where great Verulam with kindred soul could read
The Nature-mysteries that lay beneath the Pagan's creed.

LXXXIV.

A living creed to him who loves the hills
And meads where piping Pan may still be heard;
A joyous creed to him whose bosom thrills
When Philomela wakes her evening bird.
The creed of Poesy, the art divine;
Of veiled Philosophy that still must strive
To draw the diamond from the secret mine;
The creed whose winsome symbols still survive
As iridescent gems that gleam in realms that never knew
The spell that fancy wove around the bright Olympian crew.

LXXXV.

Fain would I linger in thy lap, fair Greece!
Anear the Shining Rocks in Delphi's glen;
There would I seek the navel-stone, nor cease
Until the oracles should speak again.
For Pan still lives, and they who hailed him dead,
What time with impious hands they spoiled the shrine
Of Phœbus, time hath tested and instead
Of bread they render stones and gall for wine,
While craving millions ask to see the Christ that was to come,
And failing curse the stars because the oracles are dumb.

LXXXVI.

The bitter cry of stunted souls, the wild
Ebullience of the helot, cannot these
Be lulled to sleep and man be reconciled
To live with Nature in harmonious ease?
Descend, O Pythian! as of old and bring
The bow thy ready fingers found at birth!
Draw the notched arrow to the tensive string,
And slay the dragons that lay waste the earth,
Corruption, luxury, and greed, the ethics of the mart,
That weld a golden shackle on the promptings of the heart!

LXXXVII.

Descend, O Delian! once again and guide,
As erstwhile Cretan merchantmen were led,
These later traders to Parnassus' side
And lay thy mitra on each drooping head!
So shall they rise thy priests, to immolate
The misbegotten progeny, the base
Herd of false prophets that usurp the gate
And sing for drachmæ in the marketplace.
So Competition's curse shall fail and man regenerate see
The welfare of the hive impart contentment to the bee.

LXXXVIII.

So may thy spirit, mountain land! return
And wake in us the Spartan hardihood,
The Attic ardour till our bosoms burn,
The Theban patriots' lofty brotherhood!
That we whose thoughts are moulded to the speech
To which all tongues pay tribute, may advance
The frontiers of man's commonwealth and reach
The broad savannahs where the views enhance
Our aspirations and the wide horizons merge in dim
Suggestions of new realms that lie beyond the circle's rim.

LXXXIX.

Demeter then shall see her bounteous gifts
Consigned to righteous stewards, nor abused
As pawns to justify the gamester's shifts;
The wealth of mine and factory diffused
No harpy's claws shall grapple; Labor then
Shall yield to Arrogance nor tithe nor toll;
But white-robed Peace shall come to live with men,
And love collective animate the whole:
Benevolence shall spurn the bounds of mountain, river, sea,
And kindly nations strive to win the world's hegemony.

XC.

And Art shall sit again at Nature's feet
To learn how simple are the mysteries;
And Music, Letters, Sculpture, Learning meet
Like sister children at their mother's knees.
Beauty shall flourish, every land shall own
Its thaumaturgic agency, and this
Shall turn each temple to a Parthenon,
And give each city an Acropolis
Wherein, obedient to the skill of some great master's hand,
Chryselephantine types of Love and Victory shall stand.

XCI.

And Liberty, the jewel of man's soul,
Without which life were putid, shall assume
A more than Grecian lustre and the roll
Of Aryan kinsmen shall again resume
The epic broken when the fateful pen
Within the fingers of Demosthenes
Wrote Freedom's farewell to the sons of men,
And suppliant Hellas clasped the despot's knees.
Then one great Parliament shall hold the legates of the world,
Where multitudes shall throng to see the union flag unfurled.

XCII.

And lo! as in the hero-age, the state
Of man shall then be simple: save that he
Must yield to that inexorable fate
Which none may hinder yet which all foresee,
His happiness shall be complete;—alas!
This pain supreme nor time nor love allays!
The trickling sand must dwindle in the glass,
And living is but dying; when the days
Draw near to lay the burthen down the retrospective eye
Perceives man's misery consists in knowing he must die.

XCIII.

Well spoke the sophist,[25] all that is is poured
In endless flux, the spectre stands beside
The nuptial couch, the cradle, and the board,
A silent homilist restraining pride!
The earth is but man's sepulchre[26], the whole
Great world of man may be his monument
If he but follow with unselfish soul
The path heroic where no sentiment
Obscures duty, if upon the good old Roman tree
Of civic truth he graft the shoot of Christian chivalry.

XCIV.

Lo! where the yellow Tiber sweeps the feet
Of Palatinus and the Aventine!
Pause for an instant and survey the seat
Where the three clans[27] shall gather and combine
To found the city.   This is Rome, where Force
Shall fence itself with statute and decree,
And the world's lie be sanctified; the source
Whence iron-hoofed and harsh Legality
Shall propagate its counterfeits, and Politics which spreads
The maxim that the highest good consists in counting heads.

XCV.

Patres and *Plebes*, side by side they grew,
One Roman people, yet how wide apart
In all that makes for brotherhood! the few
Born to consume and rule; the major part
Mere villeins, clods pertaining to the soil,
Winning by piecemeal every human right;
At first content to eat and sleep and toil
And read their franchise by their patrons' light!
A patient multitude well-pleased by slow degrees to rise,
And, like all patient multitudes, the slaves of Compromise!

[25] Protagoras.
[26] Thucydides, II. 43: 'Ἀνδρῶν γὰρ ἐπιφανῶν πᾶσα γῆ τάφος, κ, τ, λ,
[27] The Ramnes, Tities, and Luceres. "*Ramnenses ab Romulo, ab T. Tatio Titienses appellati; Lucerum nominis et originis causa incerta est.*" Livy, I. 13.   Yet there can be little doubt that these are primitive tribal names.

XCVI.

Yet theirs the virtues by which states increase,—
Simplicity and truth and steadfast zeal
For home and country. When the hands of Greece
Grow faint with struggling shall Rome's commonweal,
Like some great crucible, commix and blend
Competing elements and haply draw
All subject peoples to one certain end,
One common principle, the reign of law,
And perishing shall still bequeath emollients to assuage
The grim and gory truculence of the fierce iron age.

XCVII.

Leave we, twin Sisters, ye who are my guides!
These cinder heaps of Pluto where the rude
Autochthones beheld the ocean's tides
Retreat with horrid hissing unsubdued
Though neighbouring hills discharged their fiery rain,
And earth affrighted tore her rugged breast!
Forsaking these, press onward in the train
Of the great vanguard hastening to the west,
Where Partholan's[28] bronze sword doth point to Inver Sceine's head,
Or where the blue-eyed Yavana turn north with eager tread![29]

XCVIII.

First of the Keltai! draw your barques to shore,
For this is Inisfail, the Isle of Fate!
Unstep the mast and ship the guiding oar,
Behold! the Woodmen[30] resolutely wait
Within their bosky fastnesses; they bend
The supple bow and poise the flinty spear;
Wild freedom's martyrs driven to defend
Their last asylum; further flight is here
Beyond their wishes, step by step the arms of bronze have hurled
Their relics westward till they touch the confines of the world.

---

[28]Partholan, according to legend the leader of the Pelasgic Kelts, who first entered Ireland at Inver Sceine, *hodie* Bantry Bay or the Kenmare estuary.
[29]Yavana, the Young Folks, ancestors of the Germans.
[30]The forest tribes or Iberic aborigines of Europe.

XCIX.

North, east, and west, by lough and hill and glen,
Firbolg, Nemedian, tribe on tribe they spread,
Danann, Fomorian, and the later men,
Galam's Milesians with the kingly tread!
Their blood to-day flows nimbly through the veins
Of stalwart world-subduers, lo! the spark
That lighted Heremon to the fertile plains
Where gentle Barrow glides toward the dark
Child of Slieve Bloom's Silurian breast gleams faintly yet still gleams
Where the worn Maker exiled sits and mourns his youthful dreams!

C.

And Kymric blood is likewise his, perchance
Of some Cornubian Druid-bard who gave
His unarmed bosom to the Roman lance,
And fell a martyr where he might not save.
Keltic in all, the song I sing shall bear
No taint of lucre; lacking though the fire
Of loftier lays, my modest verse shall wear
No badge of service to disgrace the lyre.
Be mine the Vates' part and lot to prophesy and sing
Such soothfast words as Merlin sang before Tintagel's king!

CI.

Or he whose wizardry recalled the bloom
Of old Romance and gentle trouverie,
Whose loyal passion raised on Hallam's tomb
A stately altar to Mnemosyne.
A noble shrine where the chaste soul may learn
That sacrifice is triumph, loss is gain;
Where day and night the snowy tapers burn,
And cloistered arches echo the refrain
At evensong when anthems stir the banners like a breath,
And *Nunc Dimittis* is the heart's calm welcome unto Death.

CII.

Old Time, thou art a dullard! could'st thou not,
While sparing cromlechs, menhirs, monoliths,
Have saved the mystic lore the Druids taught,
Retained the wisdom hidden in their myths?
Then haply we had heard the tale of him,
Mysterious Hesus, whom the white-robed throng
Adored in forest temples vast and dim
With pomp and sacrifice and sacred song;
Then might the Druid's soul awake, then might his voice once more
Instruct us that man treads the paths his feet have trod before.

CIII.

What say you, brothers, ye for whom the sun
Hangs tottering o'er the western precipice?
What, brethren, if the course so nearly run
Be, as it were, a trial heat, and this
Approaching sunset but a call to sleep
Until the morrow when,—anointed, nude,
And lithe,—ye reach the threshold, fit to leap
Toward the barrier with your strength renewed?
Perchance with some faint memories of the preceding day,
Premonishments of stumbling-blocks that thwart the narrow way?

CIV.

Could captured Proteus, told to prophesy
Concerning man's hereafter, e'er reveal
A greater mystery than those which lie
Around us unregarded? Why appeal
For proofs to spheres beyond our mortal ken,
When kindly Nature spreads an open page,
And bids us read God's message unto men
Where life perennial never comes of age?
Dyes the medusa's crystal bell and bids each pulp confirm
The truth of immortality by tentacle and germ?[31]

---

[31] This thought is, in a measure, borrowed from an article by Sir Edwin Arnold, contributed, I think, to the *Fortnightly Review* some years ago.

CV.

Ah, brothers! could we stand beside the loom
Where lives are woven and take up the thread,
And know the pattern of the past, the tomb
Would be a welcome shelter to the dead!
For then the soul, re-clothed with flesh, would rise
On stepping-stones of former faults[32], and each
New birth were certain progress till the prize
Of sinless being were within man's reach;
And then, blest thought! its cycle filled, the ransomed soul would fall
A crystal drop in Heaven's sea and God be all in all.

CVI.

Gaelic or Kymric, lo! their kindred blood
Found common evolution.   Happy isles!
Where Famine came not though men understood
Nor finance nor taxation, nor the wiles
Of those who buy in cheapest marts and sell
In dearest, for whose needs the world has made
Its later ethics and abolished Hell
And every dogma that could hamper trade!
Thrice happy clansmen! who had need of little wealth beside
The flocks and herds that grazed the meads or roamed the mountain side!

CVII.

Oh! could some Poet-Druid now rehearse
The simple blessedness of far-off times,
How would men linger o'er the antique verse
And bid the modern poet turn his rimes
To loftier purpose than a roundelay,—
To sing of justice with a voice as clear
As that of some Milesian Ollamh Sai[33],
Whose counsels kings and fathers loved to hear,
Some white-haired Brehon whom his clan beheld with secret awe
Blend Filidecht and Fenechas, prophetic song and law!

---

[32] "That men may rise on stepping-stones
      Of their dead selves to higher things."   *In Memoriam.*

[33] Ollamh (pronounced *Ollauv*) Sai, nearly equivalent to Doctor of Philosophy:
an *ollamh fili* was a fully graduated poet (or *vates*); the *fenc* or lawyers as a distinct
school seem not to have preceded Christianity.

CVIII.

As with the hardy Yavana, the slow
And steadfast Germans whose determined course
From Bactria to the Baltic seemed the flow
Of some great ocean-seeker from its source,—
The kilted Gael never bent the neck
To wear the collar of imperial Rome:
Oh age of bronze and liberty! we reck
No more of Freedom than the name; her home
Hath vanished from our stagnant fens to some secluded hold
Where Lybian pigmies still evade the Christian's greed for gold.

CIX.

For us no more the life of wood and stream,
Though Nature woo us to her kindly arms!
For us, alas! the clank of wheel and beam,
With reek of furnace, where the pallid swarms
Sleep, eat, and labour, labour, eat, and sleep,
And hug the falsehood that the world has grown
Akin to Paradise when bread is cheap
And every dog contented gnaws his bone!
Where fleshly fools o'erheated rush to marriage beds and breed,
Like rodents in some crowded cage, a hasty, nerveless seed!

CX.

All-Father! give me back my lowly cot
Mid Appalachian solitudes or guide
My wearied spirit to some lonely spot,
Some other Pitcairn, hidden in the wide
Pacific's bosom, rather than prolong
This travail where dull Helots kiss the rod!
Or bid the PEOPLE rouse them and be strong
To fetter Faction! Consecrate, O God!
The new apostles of Thy Christ, let fiery tongues descend,
With Pentecostal potency bid social trespass end!

CXI.

And you, apostles of the great crusade!
Gird up your loins, for lo! the hour is nigh!
Corruption trembles, Falsehood stands dismayed,
The labarum of promise fills the sky!
"By this sign conquer!" Lo! the Church of Christ,
Her anæsthesia ended, breaks the chain
That Constantine y-forged and Henry spliced,
And God's free Spirit ranges earth again
To bid the Saxon loafward turn the ploughshare to the land,
And generous Kelts again display their pristine open hand! [30]

CXII.

The hour is nigh: Oh! well for those whose lot
'Twill be to sojourn in that blithesome world,
And share its happiness when time hath wrought
The harvest now a-ripening and unfurled
The Aryan's charter! Peace and plenty then,
With equal rights and active brotherhood,
And sweet simplicity shall bring to men
The antique joy of living with the good
Enhanced by knowledge rightly used, when Science shall employ
Her touchstone in the crucible to purge it from alloy.

CXIII.

To thee, great land! whereto my homeless heart
Was drawn what time, like Noah's dove, I flew
From seagirt Albion, could the Maker's art
Unseal the tomb and open to the view
Thy buried mysteries, then would I sing
A Past more ancient haply than the birth
Of Partholan or Heber or the king
Who learned by hunting to subdue the earth,
Nimrod, the first to demonstrate the bitter truth that might
Transcends all other claims and prove that force dictates the right!

(30) The title *lord* is said to come from *hlaford,—i. e., hlaf-weard*, or bread-keeper. From the Irish *flaith*, a tribal king, comes also *flaithcamhuil*, or open-handed hospitality.

CXIV.

Then at my bidding would the Muse disclose
The tale of that lost race whose monuments
Might hide a buried nation, or of those
Whose obelisks and sculptured pediments
And glyphs and pyramids alike defy
Time's fretful tooth and man's researches where
Palenque's, Copan's, Uxmal's walls stand high
Above the later forests; or declare
From what primæval founts Votan and Manco Capac drew
The calendar of Mexico, the tithings of Peru.

CXV.

The age of bronze o'erlaps the iron age
On Anahuac's causeway, where the fierce
Pursuing Aztecs strive with vengeful rage
To merit Huitzil's[35] favour; lo! they pierce
The hauberk and the morion and hurl
Their flinty javelins 'gainst the tempered steel;
Stone, bronze, and iron in a fiery whirl
Of blood and terror make their last appeal
To war's arbitrament, the while the teocallis flow
With gore where priests propitiate the gods of Mexico.

CXVI.

And lo! Christ's cross becomes once more the sign
Of retribution; proud Tenochtitlan
Must drain the goblet where the deadly wine
Of righteous judgment is prepared for man!
Let loose the hell-dogs! as when Carthage paid
Her awful forfeit, or as when the doom
Pronounced against Jehovah's temple made
Jerusalem a Golgotha and tomb!
Where Tophet's fiends held jubilee do Thou, O righteous God!
Pour out the vials of Thy wrath and wield Thy chastening rod!

[35]Huitzilopochtli, the Mars of the Aztec pantheon. The allusion in the text is
to the famous retreat of the Spaniards from the city.

CXVII.

From Vilcanota's slopes the reedy shore
Of Titicaca sparkles in the sun,
And Vilcamayu's rapid currents pour
A silver tribute to the Amazon.
Land of the Incas! cross and shrine in thee
Are but as dwarfed exotics, for thou art
Thyself an altar where the spheres may see
The mighty mother, Nature, lift her heart
To Him whose Thought first gave her life, where peak and torrent raise
Their *In Excelsis Gloria!* and swell their Maker's praise.

CXVIII.

Three hundred times have Cuzco's sons bewailed
And Caxamarca's maidens yearly wept
The fateful day when Athualpa[96]failed
And the great Sun-Lord's righteous vengeance slept.
Three hundred years of patience, yet the soul
Of old Peru survives the Inca's loss,
And Manco Capac's doctrines still control
A race constrained to bear the Christian's cross.
O Christ! where dark Pizarro's sword put Thee to open shame
Oppression's bitter memories still cluster round Thy name!

CXIX.

But here, where God's great mountain clusters rise,
Peak over peak in one unbroken chain,
Where Earth's perfervent furnace heats the skies,
And cloud-crowned chimneys hurl their fiery rain,
The growths of Egypt or of Palestine,—
Though nursed in Europe for a thousand years,—
Seem puny nurslings; where the Hand Divine
Withholds encouragement and Nature rears
A temple to the Unknown God and leaves the portal wide
She builds no transepts for the myths that wait on human pride.

[96]Atahualpa, the last independent Inca, barbarously murdered August 29, 1533.

CXX.

Perched on the poop of caravel and barque,
When Genoese or Briton left the shore
To find a world or refuge, stood the dark
Apollyon of the nations; swift and sure
Was Superstition's progress, like the fell
Disease the turbaned pilgrim bears abroad
From the great mosque of Mecca and the well
Of Zamzam and the stone where Ishmael trod.
And lo! the hellborn twins, Despair and Bigotry, released,
Gave Plymouth Rock and Mexico to presbyter and priest!

CXXI.

Unsightly demon! but for thee the world
Had long been blest: thou causest man to shrink,
A drivelling dotard fearing to be hurled
Through shades Tartarean when he nears the brink
Of Death's dark river! we are all thy slaves,
O Superstition! and the dædal Earth
Is septic with the odours of her graves,
While phantom shrouds envelope us from birth.
Our very mirth is overcast with fear, we frisk and play
Like sacrificial victims urged to frolic while they may.

CXXII.

The Aryan surplus, landless and oppressed,
Thy constellation tempted o'er the foam,
Great Land of Refuge! in thine ample breast
The homeless ones have found a kindly home.
And thine the duty that thou canst not shun,
And thine the guerdon of the enterprise,—
To blend the discrete elements in one,
To see the Phœnix plume her wings and rise
On widespread pinions higher than her regal parent went
The ichor from whose wounds first gave the nestling nourishment.

CXXIII.

What though the lurid and malefic star
Whose baleful light was kindled with the flame
Of this my earthly being from its far
Æthereal moorings scintillates the same
Wan presages to this new hemisphere,—
A ghastly nimbus constant to my head?
Though friends forsake me and though ties more dear
Than friendship's bonds are ruptured as a thread,
Or withered in the chilling frost of failure, not to thee
Be blame, great land whose golden hope allured me o'er the sea!

CXXIV.

A golden hope, yet not the hope of gold,
Drove me to seek thy hospitable arms;
My yearning spirit, weary of the old
Time-buttressed cheats, and tempted by the charms
Of Nature and of Freedom, turned to thee,
Nor recked of let and hindrance;—lo! the cot
My hands have builded other eyes shall see
And other feet shall rove the lawn I bought
From old Silvanus by my toil, while I regretful roam
A lonely exile shorn of strength to seek another home!

CXXV.

But yesterday the painted savage stood
Where now I stand, and saw with doubtful eye
The daring Norman[37] venture down the flood
Or marked Loyola's messenger float by.
On either hand the sea-like prairies spread
A broad expanse intact of spade or plough,
Save where some unknown barrow hid the dead
Of unremembered nations, and where now
The human tide has risen high; to-day the fertile plain
Where once the gray wolf chased the deer stands rich with ripening
    grain.

[37] Robert Cavelier, Sieur de La Salle: "Loyola's messenger." Jacques Marquette, of the Society of Jesus.

CXXVI.

Forbid it, Heaven! that this heritage
Should fall to prodigals or knaves betray!
Be this the theatre whose spacious stage
Shall show the climax of the long-drawn play
Of man's redintegration. Lo! mine eyes
Are dazzled with the vision, for I see
The commonwealth of nations take its rise
And hear the music of a world made free!
I see the prison doors unbarred, and Crime and dark Despair
Forsake their haunts like unearthed moles and breathe a purer air!

CXXVII.

Arise, imperial virgin of the west!
Arise and break the bands of ancient wrong
That odious hands have braided o'er thy breast,
Before Corruption's trammels wax too strong!
The patched and timeworn raiment of dead creeds
And systems atrophied while thou wast yet
An artless suckling cannot fit thy needs
Now that thy lissom limbs are firmly set
And thou canst wield Athena's spear and, conscious of thy might,
In white-armed majesty prepare to vindicate the right.

CXXVIII.

Thou art a debtor to the waiting world,
Whose yearning gaze has never veered from thee
Since thy great martyr's loyal hands unfurled
Redemption's charter to a race made free.
Advance thine ægis and a million brands
Shall flash responsive to thy battle call:
"Io Triumphe!" and the sordid bands
Shall flee for refuge to the donjon wall
Where Vested Interest holds his court, the citadel whose stones,
Cemented by a people's blood, are reared on human bones.

CXXIX.

Draw close the leaguer! bid the trumpet sound!
Mark how the frowning turrets sway and reel
When twice a million footsteps beat the ground
Where Freedom's warriors storm the grim Bastille!
Brief time for righteous judgment! this their hold
Shall be the caitiffs' sepulchre, a sign
For future generations when the mould
Shall gather on the ruins and the kine
Shall crop the long, lush grass and turn their deep mysterious eyes
To where some relic-hunting sage his spade and mattock plies.

CXXX.

Lo! where Urania waits upon thy star,
America! to free thy horoscope
From evil occultations: naught shall mar
Thy natal promise, harbinger of hope
To all the nations! for thou art the sure
Pledge of the coming age when Love and Truth
Shall form a golden bridge from shore to shore,
And Man regain the lusty strength of youth.
God's benison is on thy head, the blessing of thy birth
Shall follow thee till thou shalt see redemption come to earth!

 END OF BOOK II.

ADDITIONAL NOTES.

Page 26.—"Episteton," anything that can be scientifically demonstrated: that which is a subject of science.

Page 34.—"Anatocismic," i. e., by compound interest.

Page 54.—"Build up, etc.," the "silent worker" being the *corallium rubrum*, the beautiful red coral of the Mediterranean.—"Effodial relics," such as those of *elephas antiquus, elephas meridionalis*, and of still existing African types, have often been found in Sicily.

Page 55.—"The Mantuan Master,"—Virgil.

Page 61.—"Tetragrammaton," the four letters of the Hebrew Yahve (Jehovah), the I Am, or Creator.

ERRATUM:

On page 27, stanza xlv., line 6.
    For "Though" read "Through."

THOMAS CHATTERTON.

AN INQUIRY.

Ergo alte vestiga oculis, et rite, repertum,
Carpe manu: namque ipse volens facilisque sequetur,
Si te fata vocant.

(*Æneid, VI, 145-147.*)

THOMAS CHATTERTON.

AN INQUIRY.

[Thomas Chatterton (1752-1770), the boy-poet,—the most precocious and the greatest genius of the eighteenth century,—committed suicide in an obscure lodging in London on the 24th of August, 1770. "The best of his works, both in prose and verse, require no allowance to be made for the immature years of their author, when comparing him with the ablest of his contemporaries. Yet he was writing spirited satires at ten, and he produced some of the finest of his antique verse before he was sixteen years of age." (Professor Daniel Wilson, in *Ency. Brit.*) His story is the most pathetic and saddening in the mournful annals of literature.]

Εἰναι, ἥ τε δεῖ γενέσθαι ἐκ τοῦ θεοῦ, ἀδύνατον ἀποτρέψαι ἀνθρώπῳ . . . . ἡ [δίαιτα δὲ ἰδίει εν ἐστι τῶν ἐν ἀνθρώποισι αὕτη, πολλὰ φρονέοντα, μηδενὸς κρατέειν.*

(Herodotus, *Calliope*, XVI.)

I.

"Thou hast put out his glory:" lo! the psalm
Through Canyng's aisles went rolling like the cry
Of souls o'erburdened with life's mysteries
That winter eve; and I, a pilgrim, bowed
My head in acquiescence.   Then again
High o'er the organ's grounded swell I heard
That plaint continued while it told of one
Whose days of youth were shortened, and whose life
Was wrecked like some fair pinnace ere the cliffs
Of lonely Lundy bid the voyager
Take one last look at England.   Then for me
The gates of Memory were unbarred, the while
The white-robed preacher spoke his platitudes
Of God and mercy, and of life the gift
Bestowed that each might in his special sphere
Attest the Giver's goodness and augment
The Hallelujah Chorus of the world.
      Perchance the theme was threadbare, stale, or trite,

---

*"O Friend! that which is ordained of God it is impossible for man to avert...
....and the most grievous of sorrows to men is to have knowledge of many things yet be able to overcome none." (Speech of the Persian soldier to Thersander at the banquet before the battle of Platæa.)

As themes are wont to be howe'er men strive
To weave anew anachronistic threads;
Perchance my soul was in its rebel mood,
Disposed to cavil and to criticise,
Disposed perchance to question the decree
That, ere another moon should wax and wane,
Would urge me exiled from my native land.
For I was born rebellious and the hot,
Fierce blood of untamed sires filled my veins;
Of those who in the stirring times of old
Had held the Norman robber to his watch
And coward mailcoat nightly in the Pale;
Of those who led Kilmainham's shaven monks
Full many a merry dance what time they swept
The prior's cellars and the prior's board,
And seasoned foreign dainties with the rude
And keen Milesian jest; of those who wrought
Unpitying havoc on that awful day
In Cullen's Wood, ere yet the Easter hymn
Had lost its echo, while the Bristol men,
Their wives and children, kept their holiday,
And piped and feasted in the fragrant glades,
Regardless of the cruel ring that drew—
Black Monday's* doomsters—nearer and more near.
          Thus, while the parson's prosy platitudes
Fell like the drowsy hum of swarming bees
Upon my ears at evensong, my mind
Disdained the beaten turnpike where the wheels
Of that well-greased Erastian coach rolled on
In optimistic comfort, and I dared,
Before St. Mary Redcliffe's altar stone,
To ask Omnipotence its Reason Why!

---

*Black Monday—March 30, 1209, when 500 men (beside women and children) of
an English colony from Bristol were killed at Cullen's Wood, County Wicklow, by
the united septs of the O'Byrnes and O'Tooles, a deed unexpiated through six centuries of misfortune to the innocent inheritors of the wrongdoers' blood.

II.

The cosmos is a mirror wherein God
Perceives Himself, and though the human mind
Shrinks back exhausted—like some fledgling lark
First venturing to pierce the upper air—
When asked to contemplate a universe
Alike without an origin or end,
Yet none the less this Proteus-thing whose course
Is God's Procession, known alone to Him,
Hath been from Everlasting and shall be
The endless medium of His consciousness.
And every soul of man is drawn from out
The Universal Self, that so the One
Great Soul, concentred in each limited
And finite member of an infinite
Progression, may exhaust experience,
Transmuting matter everywhere to mind
By subtlest alchemy where Function fills
And heats the furnace and assimilates
Object with subject and gives birth to Thought.
Age follows age, and type succeeds to type,
But what has been shall never more resume
Its erstwhile form without variety
Or shade of difference; just as in some great
Baronial hall the curious seeker finds
The lineaments of some old cavalier
Who fought at Naseby or on Marston Moor,
Or wore his ruffles in our Virgin's court,
And gazing on some later picture marks
At once the likeness and discrepancy.
For Nature's end is progress.and she brings
Some innovation with her every turn,
Obedient to His will for whom she stands
The ready proplasm to fix His thought.
      Shall God repent Him of the thing He made
When time and conflict prove it all unfit

To bear the standard or to stand in line?
Or, as he* deemed whose lofty strain was used
To justify the order of the world,
Is all the evil that we see and feel—
The tooth carnivorous that rends and tears
The tender doe's warm flesh; the cruel beak
That stains the blossom where the mavis sung
With blood drops gushing from the songster's throat;
The whirling cloud that turns the western plain,
But now the scene of industry and peace,
Into a charnel chamber; or the dull
And muffled throb that calls the miner's wife
In wide-eyed agony to where the reek
Of the black pit-mouth marks the miner's grave;
Or in the lazar house what time the knife
And blade serrated lop his limbs away
Who drugged in mercy knows nor loss nor pain;
Or where the mother lays the flaxen head
Of the stilled prattler to her torpid breast
And in that moment dies a million deaths;
Or where the Poet, holding death aloof
By one strong purpose, sings his little song,
Perchance to reach no other ear than his,
Perchance to sound a requiem o'er his bier;—
Is all this world-pain "universal good,"
Unknown as pain to that Intelligence
To whom all Nature is an open book
Wherein His memoranda are inscribed?
Doth God not know it when the sparrow falls?
Doth He not hear him when the poor man cries?
Or when in some lone chamber Sleep descends
Through subtile vapours of mandragora
On one who, waking, found the world a hell
Of frustrate hope; or when, with hands outspread,
The victim of man's passions and the wild

*Alexander Pope in the "Essay on Man."

Defier of his social lies leaps forth
To where the kindly current whispers peace
And promised cleansing, think ye that the Eye
Beholding these hath no more sympathy
Than comes to one who with regardless foot
Hath crushed some freighted ant that crossed his path?

III.

Such questioning is all too high for me,
And feeling is a sorry base whereon
To rear an altar to the Unknown God.
And I am sick to loathing of the cant
Men call Philosophy, the endless war
Of simple thoughts made formidable by
The quack's device of poorly-mortised words
Of Hellenizing tyros in whose track
The dictionary maker groans and gleans
And daily adds a page to England's tongue.
Like to some tired truant whose best years,
Were spent in bootless wandering, who brings
Himself at last to visit the old home
In hope of rest for his declining years,
And who discovers that the petty burg
Hath lost the witchery that memory kept
Moss-shrouded in his time of pilgrimage;
E'en so I turn me to the simple creed
That in my callow youth I stood to speak,
Boxed snugly up in the old transept's pew,
What time the surpliced vicar bent his head
In solemn fealty to the eastern wall.
I turn thereto as hoping that the charm
Of whilome faith can be restored to me,
That haply I, like Naaman of old,
Retaining knowledge and experience,
May cast the sceptic leprosy and find
My childlike innocence and faith renewed.
Vain hope! as idle as the wish to turn

Back to its source the current that has passed
The moss-grown mill and bid it fill again
The slimy buckets of the ancient wheel.
      Another vicar, razored till his face
Shines like a shoat at Yuletide when the cook
Inserts a lemon in the bloodless mouth,
Now genuflects and postures in the old
Gray church whose walls have caught the ocean's spray
And worn it like a crust through centuries.
And bit by bit the pomp that priesthood loves
Is being grafted on the ordinal;
And some there are whose apprehensive heads
Are filled with bugbears and whose sermon-naps
Are fitful wanderings in a world of dreams
Where phantom parsons, chasuble encased,
Play hocus-pocus with a bit of bread.
The plain old creed that sounded sharp and clear,
At once a challenge and a battlecry,
When we his flock, followed the pastor's lead
And "I believe" came promptly from our lips,
Now drags its weary length in monotone
Like ballads chanted in the marketplace
By Munster beggars when the pigs are sold
And beery drovers, clad in shaggy frieze,
Give audience to some tale of Finn Mac Cool.
The quick thought, straining at each long-drawn clause,
Now breaks the tether and goes bounding off
O'er wide savannas, cropping here and there
Where eastern gales have borne prolific seeds
From German nurseries and specious crops
Of newer theories attract the eye.
Thus while the symbol is being slowly spun
Through half a hundred noses all the doubts
Of all the doubters of a doubting age
Obtrude unwelcome spectres, and the soul
That hoped to worship flounders in the black

Serbonian bog where every footstep takes
The stogged one farther from the stable shore.
        Where Reason stands and promulgates its No
Shall Faith step in and interpose its Yes?
It cannot be; 'twere blasphemy to deem
That He who gave the light and feeds the flame
With oil of gathered knowledge can be pleased
When the light bearer takes his little lamp
And hides it 'neath a bushel, lest its beams
Should dim the lustre of the feeble gleam
That burns before the altar and dispel
The sacred shadows where the oracles
Are heard in adumbration like a faint
Survival of the clouds of Sinai.
        The light that lighteth every child of man
Is special to himself and relative:
Envisaged through and by its tiny gleam
He makes his little world, and that to him
Is sacred Truth whose seeming to the eye
Accords with all his senses: clown or sage,
That man is trembling on the dizzy brink
Of madness who invests the things of sense
With halos and chromatic aureoles,
And peoples all the circumambient air
And space and æther with his fantasies,
As true to nature as the languid saints
Whose doll-like faces, crowned with holy hoops,
Attest the judgment of the Byzantines.
Where knowledge is denied us God exacts
No tribute of assent to mysteries.
Unable to descry the links of fate
That bind us to Necessity, we feel
A sense of freedom; let us be content
With this our independence lest we find
By questioning too closely that the law
Which bids us march to greater heights, yet leaves

Us free to venture from the beaten track
Of older pilgrims, is itself constraint.
For weal or woe we stand unto ourselves
As free to guide the current of our lives
By Reason and by Conscience, albeit
The guides themselves are vassals.   Shall we blame
The dog for fawning or essay to wean
The brute from turning round and round again
Before he seeks in Dreamland to revive
The joy of hunting? such necessity
Hangs o'er us from the cradle to the grave:
The will we boast is fashioned for us and
The drift and tenor of our little lives
Is part of one great purpose, though the book
Wherein 'tis written stands for ever sealed
To all but God, its Author and its End.

IV.

I found a lark but yestereve,
Down by the hedgerow, where the mowers leave
Unscathed by scythe one little corner where
The gate swings inward and the foxgloves share
The nook thus sheltered: there with heaving breast
          It stood beside its nest,
Stunned by the hand that did that nest bereave.

Full tenderly I smoothed its wings
And bore it to my cottage, where it sings
The livelong day, and while its little throat
Pours out its liquid melody no note
Of grief for ravished freedom strikes my ear,
          No matin song more clear
When with the sunrise all the welkin rings.

V.

O God! if that Thou art a sentient thing
And not mere feeling, why was such a mind

Permitted thus to be encaged, to beat
The cruel bars that hedged it, and at last,
Sublimely challenging the janitor
Who stands beside the portal to unlock
The ebon gate, to pass a conqueror
Or into life or silence—who shall say?
O England! on that early summer morn
The brown-armed reaper, stolid as the steer
That grazed the neighbouring pasture, stayed the hand
That drew the rasping whetstone o'er the blade,
And felt a thrill of joyance when the lark
Rose like a feathered carol overhead!
Yet who of all to whom that morning's sun
Came bright with promise in the golden fields
From Kent to Carlisle, Sennen to the Wash,
Might trace that nobler songster who had forced
His prison barriers and with ready wing
Outstripped the eagle in his haste to gain
The purer æther where no earthly taint
Or terrene element could clog his soul?
O England! where the prophet eats his bread
With salt of his own weeping, what had he,
The Boy of Bristol, common to the herd
Spoon-fingered of the greedy clowns that throng
The streets of Babylon, where burgher souls
Feel but one impulse? or of those in whom
The fire of genius heats the crucible
Where like an alchemist the student blends
Wit, wisdom, folly in his lust for gold?
Or those who, perched beneath the sounding-board,
Hebdomadally teach us to beware
Lest anchorless we drift adown the flood
To cataracts of anarchy and lust;
Who chill the lifeblood of our enterprise
And drive us skulking to the mildewed shades
Of Superstition, lest the noonday sun

Darting delirium strike our fevered heads?
    O Chatterton! if aught of thee survive
The swift obstetrics of that summer night,
Hear this my protest when I raise my voice
Disclaiming fealty to the trader's god!
Hear this my malison on that fell creed
Of contrary environment* which makes
Deformity the order of the world
And sanctifies the hemlock when man lifts
A righteous hand against the house of life!
    Brave heart and gallant spirit that could thus
Defy the Furies, snatching victory
When pitiless Megæra bade the world
Of cant and custom pile another cairn
On Genius conquered, excellence subdued,
To stand a suppliant in the servants' hall
And eat the bread of patronage or grind
A stinted measure for the Philistines
Who mock the blinded giant as he toils,
The hack of letters, for his daily crust.
Brave heart and gallant spirit! at the last
Thou madest Death thy minister and he,
Whom cowards dread and shun, became thy slave
To answer to thy summons and to tug
The labouring oar to ferry thee across
To that dim shore where thou might'st haply find
An answer to the query of thy life,
And stand before the Presence, there to learn
The secret spring of that great mystery,
Thine incarnation and thy placement in
A world inimical; to learn perchance
The reason of the union of a soul
Creative, proud, and absolute with clay
Of stolid Wessex where the yokels stand

---

*"*Antiperistasis* is a philosophical term, signifying a repulsion on every part."
(Note to Bacon's "Table of the Colours of Good and Evil.")

With mouths agape or munching lazy straws
The while they incubate their leaden thoughts.
          Brave heart and gallant spirit! who of those
Who daily drink the acid and the gall
Of cross-bound Genius while the venal scribes
Who sit in Moses' seat wag pitying heads
Hath caught no echo from that farther shore
Inviting him to venture?   Such have I
Heard in the gloaming when that Hesper, poised
Amid the changing bronzes of the west,
Shone like a beacon set at heaven's gate:
And sweeter than Æolian music seems
The murmur of the wavelets as they break
On that broad strand whereto who wills may pass
Unchallenged, unimpeded.   Bide thy time,
O ready mariner! and stand prepared
To slip thy cable when the storm of life
Blows fiercest and the rocks that fringe thy lee
Gnash deadly hatred, and the fate-spume flies
Like vipers' venom, and the wreckers wait
To see thee in the breakers while they mock
Thee struggling where the white-capped surges dash
The waifs of time upon a hostile shore.
          O welcome revolution that hath brought
Freedom to all who dare to lift their chains
And strip the rusty iron scale by scale!
And happy ye, the Christs on whom the oil
Of God's anointing truth hath been outpoured
To make ye kings, the fearless chiefs* who claim
The lordship over Self, that little realm
Where each may be a Cæsar who can dare
To challenge old Prescription and to set
At naught the greybeard Prejudice that kneels
Before the roodscreen mumbling o'er his beads!

---

*Compare Seneca, *Thyestes*, Act II.—
          "*Rex est qui metuit nihil;*
          Hoc regnum sibi quisque dat."

For weal or woe ye are the lords of life,
Imperial umpires vested with the right
Of ultimate decision: when the soul
Hath struggled through Gethsemane, and when
The grinning skulls of Golgotha shine out
In phosphorescent mockery, and when
The smirking Pharisees prepare to gloat
O'er hopeless Misery fastened to the cross,—
Then, when the skies are brazen and the air,
Surcharged with hell-fires, quivers with the glow,
And God himself withdraws within the veil
Where human plaint is heard not, then, brave souls!
'Tis yours, like Chatterton, to turn defeat
To victory most certain and to make
The Grand Inquisitor himself your slave!
Have courage, brothers! where the boy hath trod
The man may boldly follow, and perchance
Across the flood are verdant meads where songs
The sottish world refused to hear are sung
To chords that in themselves are anodynes
For all earth's pain and sorrow and neglect!
Bright fields of living asphodel where foot
Of churl or slave or caitiff never trod!
Be this our bourn, and those our comrades there
Who bore unflinchingly the stroke of fate,—
Or patriots or martyrs,—who in death
Like Saxon Harold won a nobler crown
And wider empire than the world could give!
O royal Death! O kindly Death! thy touch
Is benediction and thy kiss is sweet.

MISCELLANEA.

O, testudinis aureae
    Dulcem quae strepitum, Pieri, temperas:
      *   *   *   *   *   *
    Quod spiro et placeo (si placeo) tuum est.
        (Horat., Carm. IV, Ode iii.)

MISCELLANEA.

A CLOUD CAROL.

The Ice King wondering looked below
  Where the poet's home was seen,
At the rhododendrons' verdant glow,
The wax-leaved kalmias, row on row,
  And the mystic holly's green.

"My malison on the walls," he cried,
  "The rocky walls that fend
These sylvan dingles from my wide
Dominion and compel my pride
  And sovereignty to bend!"

He raised his hand and the hills grew pale
  At the fury of his wrath;
Vapor and cloudburst and scathing hail,
Borne on the wings of the arctic gale,
  The heralds to clear his path.

And the monarch shook from his diadem
  And scatter'd his treasures round
O'er branch and frond, o'er leaf and stem,—
Where'er he looked a twinkling gem
  That morn Hyperion found.

And lo! the Delian gave each bright
  Translucent spark a tongue:
Symbols of purity and light
Divine, they met the poet's sight,
  And this the song they sung.

   THE CIRRUS.

Over coral islets in summer seas
  We float like a fleecy veil;
In idlesse we toy with the languid breeze,

Or flirt with the joyous gale.
  And all day long
  We hear the song
Of the mighty sea, and we love to trace
Our changeful forms in his honest face.

Pure, unsullied, and chaste are we,
  Cloud-vestals in robes of snow;
Feathery, filose, and forward and free,
  High over the ebb and flow
   Of the human tide
   Of sin and pride,
Untarnished by evil, untouched by care,
We wander at will through the ambient air.

THE STRATUS.

Silently, steadily, rank on rank,
  We gather our wide array,
With tenuous squadrons on the flank
  Drawn out where the zephyrs play.

Silently, steadily, tier on tier,
  As the Titans built so build we;
And the mariner's cheek is blanched with fear
  When the shadow comes o'er the sea.

For the whilome azure tint forsakes
  The liquid dells between
The rippling crests where Triton shakes
  His locks of em'rald green.

And the leashed dogs growl in the thunder caves,
  For their time of release is nigh,
When the red bolt shoots o'er the wakening waves,
  And the lightning rends the sky.

Silently, sullenly: lo! the gale
  Is quickened and ripe for birth:—
Whirlwind and deluge and blinding hail,
  And the hurricane's frenzied mirth.

THE CUMULUS,—TORNADO.

Panting and throbbing, lo! where the city
    Heaves like a giant oppressed!
Lo! where the mother's eye looks down in pity
    On the wan babe at her breast!
  Sluggishly flows the dark river;
  Only the aspen leaves quiver;
Glaringly, flaringly gloweth the sun.—
    Oh, that his race were run!
    Oh, that the day were done!
That the jaded toilers and moilers might flee to their welcome beds,
To pray for the evening zephyr to fan their fevered heads.

    Mark ye its pulsing breast,
    Low in the far south-west,
    Where the sky and prairie meet,—
    Mark ye the spume clouds fleet!
      'Tis but a summer shower,
      Born but to die in an hour.
        Rejoice, O panting city!
        The kindly heaven in pity
          Hath sent relief:
          Pray that the storm be brief.

    Green and purple and gold,
    Gold and purple and green;
    Piling up fold on fold,
    And ever the glare between!
      Mark how the vapors throng,
      List to the storm cloud's song!

Like the small cloud that, rising from the sea,
Spread over Carmel's head its ebon pall
While Ahab rode to Jezreel, so do we
Spread darkling to the zenith: lurid all,
      Tumid and convolute,
      Pregnant with thunder:
      Lo! bird and beast are mute,
      Palsied with wonder!

Ho! for the merry dance!
Gaily we leap and prance,
Twisting and turning!
Hark! from the teeming womb
Rumbles the thunder boom
Wild lightnings burning!
          Now! now! now!
Stretch forth the finger—
Why should we linger?
          Now! now! now!

Hurrah! hurrah! hurrah!
Hurrah! for the whirlwind's breath!
          For the carnival of death!
                    Hurrah!
          Cottage and stable,
          Turret and gable,
Are food for the funnel cloud;
          Brutal and human,
          Maiden and woman,
It gathers them, humble or proud.
Hurrah for the force we wield!
Hurrah for the ravaged field!
Borne on the wild wind's wings
Lo! man and the puny things
He calleth his are sped,—
Hurrah for the stricken dead!
They are done with care and sorrow,
With the burden of to-morrow,
With the loves and hates of years,
And their meed of smiles and tears;—
          Hurrah for the peaceful dead!

The city lies prostrate, the fury hath passed,
The mourners are silent, the pale moon hath cast
Her silver effulgence in flood o'er the path
Where the Storm King went by in the might of his wrath.

The river, transfused with new life rushes by,
The fireflies kindle their lamps as they fly;
The night breeze floats in where the terror once whirled,
And whispers that death is the life of the world.

WHY?

A mother lay dead,
Dead in her prime,
And the death-watch—friends and neighbours—
Sat around;
As, in God's time,
When we, my brothers, shall have ceased our labors,
Those whom we know shall watch when that profound
Sleep that we so much dread
Shall chill our blood and turn our flesh to clay,
And dreamless night perchance shall close our day.
A mother lay dead!

One little, feeble wail,—
"Mamma!" one wailing cry:
And the guardian angel's cheek turns pale
As the accents pierce the sky.
It was her nestling-bird,
The youngest of the brood:—
O God! can it be that the cry is heard?
O God! hath the breast of the mother stirred
When the nursling cried for food?
Go to, vain man! canst thou explain
The mystery of love and pain?

BALLAD OF MINER JIM.*

1.

Write me a name and a simple line
    To tell of a noble deed;
Write me the tale of the Rossland mine;
    Write large that the world may read.

2.

Jim Hemsworth—only a common name,
    Plain Anglo-Saxon Jim:
You will find it hard on the roll of fame
    To find a place for him.

3.

Smith, Conson, Hemsworth, comrades three,
    With Jim at the windlass crank:
In that narrow shaft you might hardly see
    The daylight above at bank.

4.

They filled the bucket with gleaming ore,—
    "Stand clear!" as it rose o'erhead;
And the sturdy miners bent once more
    To the mattocks that gave them bread.

5.

Oh 'tis hard on the back and 'tis hard on the knee,
    For the shaft is deep I ween;
And a miner's winch in the north countree
    Is a clumsy, slow machine.

6.

You may strike it rich—if you're born to luck;
    You may toil from day to day
Hoping on, till you find that you've only struck
    A chute that can never pay.

*The story of "a rare act of heroism, such as deserves to be recorded in history and song, which was performed at Rossland, British Columbia," was first published (early in 1897) by the *San Francisco Examiner*, and subsequently (April 28, 1897) by the *Chicago Daily News*. At the time of writing it was not known if the hero's life could be preserved by amputating his arms at the shoulders.

7.

Two hundred dollars a month, or more,—
    You must work though you break your back;
The Chinee cook and the bill at the store,
    And the rent of the little shack.

8.

With a grip of steel in his hardened hands
    He heaves through the livelong day;
You can trace his shoulders' knotted bands
    And the rope-like sinews play.

9.

Creaking and groaning, see it come
    To the blessed upper air; ·
The cable coils round the polished drum,
    And the glistening freight is here.

10.

One effort more and the load will be
    Swung clear of the pit,—O Gòd!
See the broken crank fall aimlessly
    With the winchman to the sod!

11.

And the bucket speeds like a bolt of death
    From the light to the shaft's black gloom,
Where the awestruck diggers hold their breath
    At that rushing, certain doom.

12.

Thine hour is come: lo! Miner Jim,
    To this thing wast thou born,
As Calvary's cross came unto Him
    By whom the thorns were worn.

13.

Full on the whirling wheels he sprung,
    He thrust his arms between
Their cruel teeth, the torn flesh hung
    In shreds incarnadine.

14.

Never a cry Jim Hemsworth gave
 In his awful agony,
While the warm blood ran like a crimson wave
 From the wheels and the axle tree.

15.

Oh their hearts grew chill when the terror dropped
 On the men in that narrow mine;
But the hero smiled when the bucket stopped
 And his look was all divine.

16.

Then they blocked the wheel and with tender care
 Drew him forth from that cruel rim;
And strong men wept when they stooped to bear
 The litter of Martyr Jim.

17.

"Never mind," he cried with a cheerful voice,
 As the foreman bowed his head,
"Never mind, so long as I saved the boys;
 Thank God! they are safe," he said.

18.

Oh greater love hath no man than this,
 That he die to save his friend;
And in Love Divine he shall find the bliss
 That can never, never end.

19.

And this is the tale of the Rossland mine,
 The tale that all men should read.
And this is the name and the simple line
 To tell of a noble deed.

20.

"Jim Hemsworth, the Miner, saved his mates:"
 Be it written clear and plain;
And the world will know that the good God rates
 Jim's loss Jim's highest gain.

TO THE REPUBLIC.

Thou, with thy kingmen, every man a host
    Bucklered by Liberty, why dost thou sleep,
    While eastern breezes bear across the deep
From snow-crowned Ida and the Cuban coast
The dirge of Freedom? where is now the boast
    Of thy great charter? Lo! the angels weep
    To see thee somneous when thy sword should leap
Like vengeful lightning from its sheath: thou know'st
Thy frown can daunt the tyrant; wilt thou then,
    Oblivious of thy mission, let the stars
That grace thy standard droop in languor when
    Blood, lust, and rapine glut their greed in wars?
Oh that my call might move thee, might inspire
Thy sons once more to light the fathers' fire!

TWO AVATARS:
Buddha—Christ.

Earthward, across the gulf that spreads between
    Time and Eternity there came a Soul,—
    A life-germ from the heart of the great Whole,
And wondering shepherds, seeing its light serene,
Their flocks forsaking, guided by its sheen,
    Came, gift-beladen, to that lowly goal
    In the rude stable, where the timid foal
And wide-eyed oxen saw the wondrous scene.

O Manger-Born! methinks Thy pensive eyes
    Of introspection even now compare
This littered stable with the memories
    Of far Lumbini's pleasant garden, where
Siddhartha came the fourfold way to find
That the next avatar by Love refined.

AD SAPIENTES.

Once, in my nonage, I rode forth to quell
    Three giants grim and gory that had long
    Oppressed the nations, filled the earth with wrong,
And made man's little life a constant hell
Wherein the three fell autocrats did dwell
    Enthroned in mystery.   Trusting in my strong
    Right arm and mail of proof, I met the throng
Of hireling myrmidons and battled well.

Woe worth the day when, victory achieved,
    I called the people forth to liberty!
Then stood they blinking in the sun, aggrieved,
    Cursing the hand that dared to set them free.
And with sheathed glaive and uncouched lance I sought
A hermit's refuge in the Realm of Thought.

THE NONDESCRIPTS.

    Written after reading an estimate of the world's population,
wherein the whole human family was classed according to religion,—
as Buddhists, Christians, Mohammedans, etc.,—111,000,000 being set
down as Nondescript Heathens.

    Why stand ye thus unlabelled?   Can it be
        Ye are so worthless that Redemption passed
        Ye by unheeded? or are ye the last
    Reserve of the great army, doomed to see

    Christian and Moslem, Buddhist, Brahman fling
        The temple idols into one vast heap
        Conglomerate, that haply they may keep
    Each its own interest in the smelted thing?

    Then while men marvel that their god should be
        A senseless, dumb alloy, will ye reclaim
        The creed primæval, and perchance proclaim
    The primal truth that God has made man free?

THE CRY OF GREECE.
(April, 1897.)

O Wingless Victory!* come forth and stand
    Where stood thy temple in the days of old!
    Come forth to shame the caitiffs who withhold
Their help and comfort while the hellish band,
Mahound's blood drinkers, desolate the land!
    Shame on thee, England! that thy lust of gold
    Hath closed thine ears while God himself hath tolled
The knell of Turkish infamy! Thy hand
Could stay the mongrel crew and rescue Greece.
    How art thou fallen from thy high estate,
That for thyself thou seek'st ignoble peace,
    Taking thy cue from despots, whose vile hate
Of Hellas and her hopes portends for thee
An empire lost and lapsed supremacy!

GAUTAMA BUDDHA.

Thou wast a living, breathing man, with heart
    Attuned like mine to every human chord;
    Feeling the needs that I feel, drawn toward
Wife, offspring, friends, and country; and thou art
Man's best exemplar in the allotted part
    We all must play in life, where no reward
    Is higher than the meed of being lord
Of that small realm where Passion's fiery dart
Makes living misery. Oh! would that I
    Could follow in thy footsteps and attain
The heights serene to view the tranquil sky
    Where not an echo of earth's cry of pain
Disturbs the æther, so might I combine
Thy spirit's freedom and thy love divine!

*Nike Apteros, whose temple on the Acropolis commemorated the victory over the Persians near the river Eurymedon.

THE SENTINEL.*

He stands at the door, yet he enters not,
    That sentinel old and grim;
Nor princeling nor satrap meeteth aught
    Of sign or salute from him,
        As they pass him by
        With averted eye;
But their cheeks grow pale and the quick nerves thrill
At thought of that Presence so cold and still.

He hath stood long syne on the snowy plain
    Through many a weary day,
And heard unmoved the slow refrain
    As the exiles went their way;
        And ever I ween
        That scythe so keen,
When in pity swung for the exiles' groans,
Hath left but the stubble of whitened bones.

Full oft hath he passed by the fortress wall
    And hath heard the bitter cry;
And unheeding sped beyond the call
    Of the wretch who fain would die.
        In the land-thrall's cot
        He may gather not,
But the landlord's wealth and the landlord's state
Turn to dust at his knock on the castle gate.

He stands at the door of the mighty Czar
    And counteth the grains of sand;
When the last shall fall nor bolt nor bar
    Shall make him stay his hand.
        Grim sentinel!
        Could'st thou but tell
To the waiting millions o'er all the earth
That this vigil of Death meant a people's birth!

*Written during the last illness of Alexander III., Czar of Russia.

LOVE'S STAGES.

How doth he love who loves in youth?
With fondest trust and vows of truth;
Ere passion taints, his love is sooth—
      Abiding.

How loves the maid when fancy's wing
Of new-born faculty doth spring
To greet bright Eros as her king?
      —Confiding.

How loveth he to whom the years
Of manhood's toil and manhood's tears
Have given judgment, strength, and fears?
      —Right surely.

And she whose youthful years have fled,—
How loves she when from out the dead
Dust of past hopes a spark is bred?
      —Demurely.

For him who feebly strives to throw
On autumn leaves Love's æstive glow
How shines the taper burning low?
      —Obscurely.

Oh world-renewing, mighty Love!
Like the branch brought by Noah's dove
Thou bringest pledges from above
      To allure me.

What though Time's frost hath touched my brow,
What though the furrows of his plough
Are on my cheek? yet will I vow
      As lightly

As when in youth I swore to be
The slave of Beauty—age shall see
The silvery flame alive in me
      Burn brightly.

And when my barque floats on the wide
Dark river, and I feel her glide
To where Oblivion's silent tide
　　　　Heaves never,—

Then let me bear across the sea
To shores unknown one memory;
That woman's love may comfort me
　　　　For ever!

TOO LATE.

Thou canst not call it back:
　　　Though done but yesterday
　　　It evermore shall stay
A deed wrought by thy hand,
Whose consequence shall stand
　　　For ever and for ever,
　　　Retrieve it shalt thou never:
Thou canst not call it back.

Thou canst not call it back:
　　　Although in after years
　　　Thine eyes distil salt tears,
When memory shall recall
The story of that fall,—
　　　A trusting maid,
　　　A love betrayed:
Thou canst not call it back.

Thou canst not call it back:
　　　Repentance cannot bring
　　　Exemption from the sting;
Remorse shall weigh thee down
In field or tower or town;
　　　The wide world o'er
　　　It goes before:
Thou canst not call it back.

Thou canst not call it back:
>   Not though thy voice could reach
>   Where never human speech
> Or human sigh was heard,
> Whose calm was never stirred,
>   Where all is naught
>   But God's own thought:
> Thou canst not call it back.

Thou canst not call it back:
>   Standing beside her tomb,
>   Be this thine awful doom,
> To know 'twas done for aye—
> Sought, yielded, cast away!
>   One little heart
>   Giv'n, torn apart:
> Thou canst not call it back.

Thou canst not call it back:
>   Not though her spirit bore
>   Forgiveness from the shore
> Too early sought, when love
> Was outraged; far above
>   All form of will
>   The Past stands still:
> Thou canst not call it back.

Thou canst not call it back:
>   Not even when thy soul
>   Shall reach its final goal,
> And in the clear white light
> Of that All-Searching sight
>   Archangels read
>   Aloud that deed,
> Thou canst not call it back.

Thou canst not call it back:
>   Within the eternal gates
>   Silent her spirit waits

Thy coming;—how wilt thou,
With falsehood on thy brow,
In thy great need
Find grace to plead?
Thou canst not call it back.
Miserere, miserere
Mei, Domine!

RICHARD REALF.

(Died Oct. 28, 1878. Buried in Lone Mountain Cemetery, San Francisco.)

There, within hearing of the mighty sea,
They made thy bed, O Gifted One! and raised
Thy simple monument, where love erased
All mention of the curse that fell on thee
When thou, Apollo's envoy, bent thy knee
Where loose-zoned nymphs and graces passion-crazed
Attend Cythera's chariot.* When, amazed,
We saw thee break the lute whose melody
Had charmed two hemispheres, and when thy soul,
In terror flying from its Nemesis,
Had rushed unbidden to that unknown goal
Where she was waiting thee whose fiery kiss
Made thee a man and exile, then we learned
How bright the flame men called thy Genius burned.

*Horat, Od., lib. I, Ode 30.

AT GOLDSMITH'S GRAVE.*

London, October 31, 1894.

I.

All-Hallow-Eve and Goldsmith's humble grave!
    Beyond me, like the distant roar
    Of western surges on the shore
Where the black Longships snarling meet the wave
    I hear the din of Fleet Street, and within
    The Templars' church the choristers begin
The chant that on the morn shall fill the nave
    And gray rotunda with a silver flood
    Of melody and praise as when the blood
Of the stern warrior-saints who gladly gave
    Their all to Christ was stirred,
    When the proud psalm was heard
On eastern deserts where the paynim horde
First learned to dread the Templar's hymn and sword.

II.

My years have number'd his, and lo! I stand
    By Goldsmith's grave at Hallow-E'en!
    Patience, my spirit, while I glean
Time's aftermath within my ready hand!
    Enduring, humble, hopeful, this was he:
    This, too, All-wise Disposer! teach thou me,
Forgotten pilgrim to my native land!
    Here, where the very pavement hath a voice,
    I hear a whisper bidding me rejoice
To bear the standard of the knightly band
    Who, strengthened by defeat,
    Unflinchingly can meet
The barbed arrows of the Paynim throng
Who scorn the minor poet and his song.

*First published in the *Religio-Philosophical Journal.*

RICARDO ANTONIO PROCTOR.

VIRO PRÆDITO VIRTUTE MNEMOSYNON.

The murmuring rill in ocean finds its death,
     So glides man's life toward the gloomy portal,
     Alas! how speedily of every mortal
The memory fades, as fades the parting breath.*

To nobly live the sage's life resigned,
     For human good its calm career pursuing—
     Or nobly die for man and man's well-doing,
Alike becomes and proves the generous mind.†

Inspired and cheered by all who knew its worth,—
     The hope of fame with altruism blending—
     Such Proctor's life, whose all-unlooked for ending
Awoke a chord of sorrow round the earth.

No fav'rer he of mysteries profound;
     His keen eye searched the cosmos to discover
     Its hidden meanings, while of truth a lover
He scorned to feign when angry bigots frowned.

In him reviv'd, we saw the generous fire
     That glowed in Bruno's gallant bosom burning;
     From Falsehood's compromise with horror turning,
As Bruno spurned the image from the pyre.‡

---

* δεῖ, τοῦ θανόντος ὡς ταχεῖά τις βροτοῖς
   χάρις διαρρεῖ—Sophocles, AJAX, 1266-7
† ἀλλ' ἢ καλῶς ζῆν, ἢ καλῶς τεθνηκέναι,
   τὸν εὐγενῆ χρή.—Ibid 479 80

‡In 1875, Mr. Proctor, upon being informed that certain of his scientific opinions and teachings were opposed to the doctrines of his church, unreservedly abjured and withdrew from that church. In 1878, when a well-known London minister alluded to the terrible loss of life resulting from the sinking of the *Princess Alice*, as an example of God's mercy to the survivors, Mr. Proctor and the writer of these lines entered forcible protests against such pulpit utterances. In one of his letters on this occasion, Mr. Proctor wrote thus: "No wonder clergymen complain that Atheism, or what they take to be Atheism, is spreading. Better a hundred-fold to believe in no God at all, than to believe in such a God as some of them picture to us." (From *The Open Court*, Sept. 27, 1888.)

Thrice noble Indagator! thou shalt live
    In minds whose *form* is partly thine,—preparing
    The way to "vaster issues," still declaring
The glory of the bounty God doth give!

God—the Eternal Order—Being—All:
    Of whom we are, in whom we shall be ever;
    Changing through all, but deviating never,
Though suns grow dark, men die, or sparrows fall.

THE CARDIOGRAPH.*

(Suggested by 1887 being the Fiftieth Anniversary of the Invention of
the Electric Telegraph.)

    Said Cupid to Venus:
    "Dear mother, between us
I think we can hit on a notion,
That will give us much pleasure, and serve in a measure
    To keep all mankind in commotion.

    "A creature called Morse,
    A Yankee, of course;
The devil's in all of that nation—
Has struck an invention, of which I've heard mention,
    Which certainly beats all creation.

    "With wires and dials,
    And magnets and phials,
Men chatter together at ease,
From Boston to Cork, San Francisco, New York,
    Over deserts, through rivers, and seas.

    "Shame befall us if they,
    Mere creatures of clay,
At us, the Immortals, should laugh!
So let us be wise, and something devise,
    To rival the new telegraph."

---

*First published in Chicago *Morning News*, June 8, 1887.

Thus spoke the boy Cupid,
Whom some gods thought stupid:
And, lo! in a moment he found·
An energy latent, Jove granted a patent,
With powers to test it around.

With his bow in his hand,
The blind boy took his stand,
Not far from two children of earth:
He touched both their hearts with the point of his darts,
And flew back to heaven in mirth.

And since then, each heart,
However apart
In distance—holds commune most sweet;
For, though oceans should run between them, each one
Feels the other responsively beat.

MY MOTHER.
April 26, 1865.

Thou, I, and God's own priest,
And that clear April morn;
The dedicated feast—
And lo! thou wast reborn!

Then stood I there alone,
Alone henceforth to be;
A helmless vessel thrown
A waif on life's black sea.

Oh! piteous hands that reach
Beyond the veil in vain!
Oh! grief too deep for speech!
Oh! heritage of pain!

FINIS.

Publisher's Notice.

A limited number of copies of this volume has been re-served to meet the demand that may result from reviews and press notices. With these exceptions, the first edition has already been sold. Single copies can be secured only from the author,

243 Fifth Street, La Salle, Illinois, U. S.,

at the following prices, including postage:

U. S. and Canada	One Dollar.
Great Britain	Four Shillings.
France	Five Francs.
Germany	Four Marks.
India	Two Rupees.
Japan	One Yen.

The author of "Song of the Ages" earnestly requests that a copy of every review or notice may be mailed to him. This favor is especially solicited from journals published outside the United States.